# MEANT TO FLY

A BIRDS OF BOSTON NOVELLA

## S. E. EMORY

## —BIRDS OF BOSTON SERIES—

*Chasing Phoenix — Leo & Everett*

*Finding Raven — Colette & Gage*

*Meant to Fly — Millie & Ski*

*Saving Sparrow — Natasha & Hale*

"Don't Take The Girl" | Tim McGraw

"Falling Like The Stars" | James Arthur

"How Long Will I love You" | Ellie Goulding

"Can't Help Falling in Love" | Kina Grannis

"Like I'm Gonna Lose You" | Jasmine Thompson

"You Are The Reason" | Calum Scott

For Grandpa Ski

Thank you for introducing me to coffee. With every sip, I remember those mornings with you.

-S

**Gówno** - Shit

**Tato**– Papa

**Księżniczka**– "Share-enz-niche-ka" – Princess

**Wiatr pod moimi skrzydłami**— The wind under my wings

**zostaw ją w spokoju**— leave her alone

**Dziękuję Bogu za jedzenie, rodzinę... i nowych przyjaciół. Jedzmy**— I thank God for food, family... and new friends. Let's eat

**księżniczka nie jest przyzwyczajona do tak prostego jedzenia**—The princess is not used to such simple food

**Cisza**— Silence

**Szalona starsza pani**— Crazy old lady

**Nie okłamuj jej**— Don't lie to her.

**Trzymaj się z daleka od tego, tato**—Stay out of this, papa

**Tato! Zamknij się, proszę**—Dad! Please shut up!

**Jesteś dla mnie takim wrzodem na dupie**— You're such a pain in my ass.

"Some people spend an entire lifetime wondering if they made a difference in the world. But, the Marines don't have that problem."

—— Ronald Reagan

# millie

The fair is in town, finally! I have been waiting for months, and it's finally here. My favorite time of year. Not only is it my birthday today but July also brings in the fair for a couple of months. A couple of months of games, rides, salty popcorn, and cheap prizes.

My friends and I are at the fair almost every night until school begins and then every weekend until it leaves in September. I love escaping and feeling like a normal girl.

I'm not the mayor's daughter. I'm not the ballet dancer meant to be a prima one day. I'm not the captain of the cheer squad. I'm not the valedictorian. I'm just a girl with her friends.

But even better than that, Daddy will be home tonight. He promised when he left two weeks ago that he would be home in time to celebrate my fourteenth birthday. He always makes it home for my birthday. It's been two weeks since I've seen him last, and I miss him terribly.

I know his job is important, but he is always away, and Mama is always with him.

*"It's important to appear as a well-rounded, united front. That is why your mother must accompany me, my beautiful doll. And one day, when you are old enough, you will join us."*

Daddy told me that when I was eight, and I begged them not to leave... again.

But that was years ago, and I'm still left behind. Always left behind. I have to admit, I'm not that close with Mama, so her presence isn't as missed. She has always pressured me more than Daddy. Trying to shape me into a "proper lady."

Really, Mrs. Evelyn is the one who has raised me all my life and acted as a mother. She stays behind when they leave. But no matter, he is coming home tonight.

He will be here.

Tying up half of my long blonde hair with a pink ribbon, I twirl in front of the mirror. Daddy sent me this dress for my birthday, and I can't wait until he sees me in it.

The rounded neckline has a small bow right in the middle and the pink skirt is pleated at the waist, it flares out slightly and hits below my knee. I pair it with my white oxfords and socks with ruffles also courtesy of my father. I clip on my pearl earrings and matching necklace and remember the day my mama gave them to me.

*"A lady always needs her pearls, Millie dear. It's what sophisticated women wear. It's how we show who we are and where we belong. Never forget them. I don't care if you still have curlers in your hair, or you're in your finest dress, you must always have your pearls."*

I lean down in front of my vanity and put a little rouge on my cheeks and lips to add color. My skin is so fair, and I hate it. All the other girls are tan in the summer, the New York sun makes them glow. But not me. I just get a nasty sunburn, then peel back to my fair skin. But I do love my big blue eyes. I think that's why Daddy calls me his doll—fair skin, blue eyes, long blonde hair.

"Miss Millie, you have someone at the door for you," Mrs. Evelyn calls up from the bottom of the grand staircase.

Daddy is finally home! My dress flutters as I race down the stairs, but I stop abruptly when I see it's just Christian and Marryanne.

"Oh. Hello." Disappointment leaks from my voice, but I can't help it. Their eyes meet mine, and I know based on the pitiful looks they give me that they know exactly who I thought they were.

"They aren't home yet?" Marryanne, my best friend since third grade, says as she comes up and embraces me in a small hug, barely touching to keep her appearance in place. Her dark curly hair, stiff from her hair spray, practically suffocates me. Goodness, how much hair spray did she use?

Pulling away, I brush down my dress and fix my hair. "No. But there is still time. My daddy is always home for my birthday."

Christian comes up to my other side, opposite Marryanne, and lays a hand on my lower back. "Well, if he doesn't make it, we will be here."

My lips pull up in a sad smile. "Thank you, Christian. But he'll be here. He always makes it."

"Are you ready to head out?" Mrs. Evelyn steps up to the front door, curlers and scarf in place atop her head. Already ready for bed.

I can't help but feel the defeat in my heart. I know better than anyone not to get my hopes up. But it's my birthday. He's always here for this night. Even when he has missed other events, like my first ballet recital, my first day of junior high, the day I won the spelling bee... he has *never* missed my birthday.

Maybe the only one I can truly rely on is my nanny. She has always been there. Even as nice as my friends are to me, sometimes I wonder if it's me they love or my family name.

We all climb into the back of the car as Mrs. Evelyn starts it up, the engine roaring and the smell of the exhaust filling the air. The leather seats squeak beneath us, and then we're off.

As we pull up to the fairgrounds, the car rocks as it rolls over the potholes. Mrs. Evelyn turns down the radio, silencing Eddie Holland's "Where Did Our Love Go," most likely to give us our "talking-to" she is obligated to recite.

"Okay now, children, remember to stay together, don't go runnin' off with any strangers, and I will be here, right here at eleven o'clock sharp. Don't be late, or I'll go in after ya and pull ya out by your ears."

The thrill of what is to come excites me, and I begin to tune her out.

"Are you listening?" she reprimands as all our heads snap to her.

"Yes, ma'am," we say in unison as we slide out of the new teal-and-white car that my mama just picked out but has yet to drive herself. I don't even know what kind it is, but whatever it is, I'm sure it costs a pretty penny. Mama doesn't buy anything cheap.

As soon as we are through the ticket booth, Marryanne grabs my hand and drags me toward the first ride. Loaded into the swings, they lift and spin us round and round. The wind through my hair makes me feel like I'm flying. I throw my arms out wide and laugh until my stomach hurts.

Then I go on the Ferris wheel, where I feel like I can see the entire world. Everything seems so large and problematic when you're on the ground, but up here? It's all so small. All your worries and problems seem a little less daunting when you're flying high in the air.

Finally, we load up on cotton candy and begin playing the games. I see the exact teddy bear I want. It's practically as big as I am. Light brown with a white ribbon tied around its neck in a big bow. It's perfect.

Some might think a fourteen-year-old wanting a giant teddy bear is childish, but not to me. Ever since I was eight, my daddy has taken me to the fair on my birthday and won me a teddy bear. It's our thing. I have all my bears lined up on my window bench seat. From the first to the most recent, those bears mean more than anything to me. It's something he does for me and me alone, and it's special.

But not this year. I know he isn't going to make it this year.

My friends play the games, winning little prizes, and I just stare at the bear. Like it's mocking me. Laughing at me for tearing up over a stuffed animal.

But I can't help it.

I miss my daddy.

When he is home, he's my best friend. He's the best dad in the world.

When he's home, that is. And I understand he has a big, important job. I was raised to understand, but my birthday and this fair and that teddy bear are our thing. It's the one night in my life when I am important to him.

The tears begin to fall, and I'm too ashamed to admit to any of it because it's stupid really. I have everything I could ever want, except parents who are there for me. Why would the princess of Ridge Port, New York, be crying? What could possibly be wrong in her life?

As the tears begin to fill my eyes, I back away and head to the back of the concession stand. I just need to be alone for a minute, to collect myself so I can go back out there and be happy for everyone.

*Ping.*

*Ping.*

*Ping, ping.*

A tin can comes flying at my face, and I quickly duck to avoid getting hit.

"Oh gówno!" A boy, about my age, comes jogging up to me, tucking something in his back pocket. "I'm sorry, I didn't mean to almost hit you. Are you okay?"

How does he know he didn't hit me? Careless boy. Just what I need right now. "Well, you did!" I exclaim as I wipe away my tears. Now not only am I heartbroken but I'm also embarrassed. I didn't want him to know I was crying, but I can't hide it the closer he gets.

He reaches up and pushes away a piece of my hair that had fallen into my eyes. "Why you crying? Did I hurt you?"

"No. No. I just..." Straightening out my skirt and fluffing my hair, I do my best to look my best. Just as Mama always says. But then I take in the boy. I think I recognize him from school, but I can't be sure. He's so... dirty.

His dark brown hair is disheveled, his white shirt and brown trousers are covered in stains, and one of his shoes has a hole in it, the sole separating from the leather in the other. His pants are about two sizes too big on his slight frame. The dirt under his nails and the light brown sheen against his skin tells me he hasn't had a proper bath in who knows how long.

But... under all that, his eyes glow. The blue reminds me of glaciers in the dark water, like a beacon in the night. His lips are full, and he has high cheekbones that any girl would kill for. He's... dare I say, handsome. But he could still use a bath.

"I—you didn't hurt me. I'm fine."

"Well then why were you crying for?" he asks again.

Nosy much? He doesn't even know my name. But something warm about him draws out my willingness to share. "You'll think it's silly."

He just shrugs one of his shoulders and turns away from me, "Well, you can go ahead and cry if you need to. I get it. Just watch out." Pulling out a little rubber band gun from his back pocket, he aims it at the tin cans that I now see are lined up on a log behind the concession stand.

"Wait, you don't want me to tell you?" Stepping back, the gravel crunching beneath my shoes, I watch as he hits three cans in a row, one right after the other.

*Ping. Ping. Ping.*

He's pretty good at that.

"Nah. If you think it's silly, it probably is."

I should turn around and walk away, but something about him makes me stay. Walking over to him, I run my hands down the back of my thighs, tucking my skirt as I sit on an old wooden crate next to him.

"Well, it's probably silly to you, but it means something to me."

He fires off a few more shots. His aim is incredible. I can barely see the cans in the dark night, but he hits them without even breaking a sweat.

"Tell me or don't. It's up to you. I'm not gonna bother ya 'bout it."

"I didn't get a teddy bear that I was really wanting." I blurted it out, not even meaning to. But I just want to keep talking to him. Keep him talking really. His voice is calming. Soothing in a way that I've never experienced before. There is a quietness about him that I appreciate. He isn't vying for my attention or looking for me to be anything other than comfortable.

"Huh?" He looks down at me like he's confused, his brows crinkling in and forming a cute little dimple between them.

"I was looking forward to getting one of those giant teddy bears... you know, the one with the white ribbon... from that shooting game... I-I didn't get it like I thought I was going to."

*Ping.*

He hits another can. Not even looking at me anymore.

"What a księżniczka," he mumbles.

*Never mind. He can shut up now.*

"Excuse me?" I stand, anger urging my legs to move and cross my arms over my chest. He just seemed so nice a second ago. What's changed?

"You mean to tell me all those tears were because you didn't get a stupid bear?" He still hasn't looked my way, just focusing on his stupid tin cans.

I stomp my foot, trying to get him to look at me. "Well, that bear meant a lot to me."

"I get it. Spoiled little brats put all their hopes and dreams into silly little things because they have everything else in life, right? Now you don't get what you want, and the world is ending." He scoffs and shakes his head.

*Still* not looking at me.

Why won't he look at me? Everyone always looks at me.

"Well, I'd rather be a spoiled little brat who puts her hopes and dreams into silly little things than a stinky boy who only knows how to shoot things!"

Turning on my heel, I stomp off. Stupid boy. He doesn't know what he's talking about!

"Bye, księżniczka!" he hollers out, and I spin back to him. Leaning down, I pick up a rock and throw it at him as hard as I can. "I'll show you a...whatever the hell you just said!"

He easily dodges the rock, laughing as he does, and I begin to stomp toward him. I'm seriously going to—

"There you are!" Marryanne calls, and then she is wrapping me in her arms. "We couldn't find you anywhere."

"Yeah, Millie, we thought someone might have taken you. Don't scare us like that again." Christian comes up and turns me away from the boy. He's lucky my friends found me, or I would have found a new and creative way to shove my pretty white Oxford up his you-know-what. Stupid, stinky boy.

"I'm fine. Let's just go," I huff out, and they don't argue.

## Chapter Two

"Millie. Wake up, sweetie. Time for school." My mom's musical voice invades my dream about a certain boy shooting cans.

"Hmmm," I groan. "Just a few more minutes." Taking the pink covers in my hands, I flip them over my head in an attempt to drown out all things morning.

"No. No. It's your first day. We must take extra time this morning with your hair and outfit. First impressions are everything. You know this. Now up before I go get Mrs. Evelyn."

The threat forces me to flip my covers off faster than a greased pig. "I'm up!" I cannot have her drenching me in ice-cold water this morning. Although if you ask Mama, she would say the ice bath is good for my skin. Well, Mama, it ain't good for my sanity.

"Come." She beckons me to my vanity, where she has my ribbons laid out, rouge already open and ready, and my white blouse and purple and gold plaid skirt hung. My Oxfords and white knee socks sit on the wooden chest at the end of my bed.

As I sit on the bench before my vanity, Mama begins undoing my curlers, then begins brushing out my long blonde hair.

"Remember to be polite to all your teachers. Don't look at the floor when you walk and touch up your rouge after gym."

"Mama, I know." I roll my eyes, and she gives a tug to my hair. "Ouch." I glare at her through the mirror.

"Manners."

"Sorry." If she detected my sarcasm, she didn't say anything.

"I called Principal McGivens and had your schedule adjusted so you have gym at the end of the day. But you still must be presentable for your after-school programs. I've signed you up for student council. You should plan to run for class president. Then you have cheer. Normally, the two have time conflicts as they are both directly after school. However, they have made an exception for you. You will practice with the cheer coach independently following student council."

Her flawless, delicate hands grab the purple ribbon from my vanity, and she begins to pull my hair half up.

"That's... I'm going to be extremely busy, Mama. None of my friends are involved in that much at school. Why do I have to be?"

She tugs at the ribbon, pulling at my hair. I wince but don't say anything as she fixes the bow, making it perfectly proportional.

"You are not like other girls."

*Don't I know it.*

"This is not up for discussion. You will participate in both extracurriculars, and you are still expected to maintain your 4.0 GPA.

Ivy Leagues will be looking not only at your grades but also at what you do outside of the classroom."

"Mama, those colleges don't even admit women. Your expectations are too high."

The light pink rouge I apply to my cheeks complements the purple of my ribbon and skirt. "You need more rouge. I'll let Mrs. Evelyn know to pick some up at the market. And they don't admit women *yet*." She enunciates the yet, implying that as soon as it's permitted, I'll be required to apply. "But there is talk of women attending Ivy Leagues soon. By the time you are ready for college, they will be. I'm sure of it. And we must be prepared."

Ushering me out of my stool, she motions me to my uniform. "Now dress and meet me downstairs."

"Yes, Mama."

Just before closing my door, she turns, and I find myself hoping for understanding, a compliment, heck, even an "I love you."

Her eyes look me up and down. "And don't forget your pearls."

"Yes, Mama." I bow my head as I button up my blouse. Upon the click of the door, I drop my shoulders and relax my posture.

By the time I make it downstairs, Mrs. Evelyn has prepared breakfast, and Daddy sits at the table with a newspaper, already dressed in his charcoal-gray suit. Mama floats around the house, freshening up the flowers in the vases and moving her small trinkets. She does this when she's nervous, but I couldn't say what she could ever be anxious about.

"Good morning, doll. How did you sleep?" Daddy takes a bite of his toast, following it with a sip of coffee.

Leaning in, I place a soft kiss on his cheek. "I slept well, Daddy. Did the rally go well in Boston yesterday?"

"It did, sweetie. Your mother told me you wanted to do student council and cheer this year. Don't put too much on your plate, doll. You still must be able to maintain your grades."

I glance at Mama, who glances back at me with a look that says to hush my mouth.

"Yes. I believe I can handle it. Colleges will be looking at not only my performance in the classroom but outside of it as well."

"Smart girl." He gives me a smirk, and I beam with pride.

"Up, up. We must get going." Mrs. Evelyn rushes me.

"But I didn't get to finish—"

"In the car, young lady. Maybe if you didn't spend so much time on that hair, you would have been able to eat a full breakfast."

"Ugh! You lot are so difficult!" I protest, and they all just roll their eyes at me.

"Love you, doll."

"Have a nice day! Mind your manners!" Mama shouts at the same time.

And off we go. Time to miserably fail at meeting expectations.

The large brick building and stone steps are a welcomed sight. Because as much as I complain about school, I do love being here. There is no expectation to be more than just a girl. Can my friends be a bit superficial? Yes. But they still make me laugh and smile. They listen when I complain about my parents.

In every way they know how to be, they are there for me. I'm not stupid. I know that if I wasn't the mayor's daughter, I probably wouldn't have the friends I do, but I can't change that. I am who I am, and I'm not going to turn away people who want to be there for me, even if they are only there for my name and popularity. Surrounding myself with people is how I distract myself from the loneliness of home.

"Millie!" Marryanne runs up to the car, opening the door before I even have the chance to. I wave to our driver, who usually accompanies Mama and Daddy, and blow a kiss to Mrs. Evelyn, who blows one back.

"What has you so excited this morning?" I question as she bounces up and down, barely able to keep her books in her bag.

"It's our freshman year! I already picked up your schedule, and we have four classes together this year!

"Four? Are you sure that's right?" Snatching the schedule she holds out to me from her hands, I look it over, and then I glance at hers.

Unfortunately, she is right. What cruel God did I piss off to let this happen?

Yes, she is my best friend, but she is the type of person I can only take so much of in twenty-four hours.

"Yay," I say with little enthusiasm, and she just giggles, thinking I'm kidding.

But I'm not.

As we walk up the steps, I notice the boy from the fair at his locker. He is in the same clothes he was in a few weeks ago. At least they look the same. The slacks and white collared shirt are just as dirty as they were then, and I wonder if he washed them at all or if the stains run so deep, no amount of soap could relieve them of the clothing.

Marryanne and I stop at our assigned lockers, and of course, hers is right next to mine. We came on Friday to set up our lockers so everything we need is already there. Which is nice since first days are already a little hectic.

I hear her fumbling with the lock, and finally, she gets it open. "Earth to Millie?"

I didn't realize I was still staring at that boy. Oops.

As if he could feel my eyes on him, he looks my way. His blue irises crash into my own, and the smirk that graces his face makes butterflies erupt in my stomach. But then he turns away, and I... wait. Why didn't he come say hello?

Not that I would admit it out loud, but he has been on my mind since I had my extremely frustrating interaction with him a few weeks ago. But it's only because I never got a chance to tell him how I really felt about his attitude toward me.

*Yeah, Mills. That's the reason...*

"Who is that?" I ask no one particular as I watch him walk away.

"Who?" Christian asks as he approaches and follows my stare.

"That's Henry... Cow-saki or something. I don't know. Some weird Polish name."

Turning away from Henry, I open my locker and am almost taken out by a giant teddy bear with a white ribbon around its neck. The same one that was at the shooting game stand at the fair. "Oh my God."

"Hey, your dad got you that bear after all. How did he get it here?"

"I-I don't know," I whisper because it wasn't my dad. I look over my shoulder to find Henry walking down the hall.

As we walk to our homeroom, I continue to watch him. He ducks into room 104, which happens to be the same room Christian, Marryanne, and I are going to.

"Why would someone show up at school in dirty rags? Like at least wash your clothes if you aren't going to wash your body." Marryanne sneers at him as we take our seats in the front. He is hiding in the back, and although I'm sure he heard her since she made no attempts to say it quietly, he doesn't say a word back to her.

But I will. "Don't say that. You don't know his story."

"Please. Everyone has access to water. You have to, or you would die. Anyone can wash their clothes." Rolling her eyes, she begins pulling out her materials for class. Glancing back at him, I watch as he just bounces his pencil steadily on top of the desk, busying his hands.

"I heard his mom died. He has like a million brothers, and they all live in this little shack in the Shanty District. Kinda sad," Christian remarks.

"So it's just his dad and his brothers then?"

"Yeah. His dad works in the mines. I overheard my dad talking about their situation once. He had to ask my dad for an advance on his paycheck for some reason. I don't know. I just know they all look like that. Rags for clothes and always dirty. God, can you imagine what his house looks like if that's what he presents himself like at school?" Christian scoffs and turns to his backpack to pull out his materials.

The notebook I take out is new and pristine, without a single mark on it, but the paper Henry takes out is all crumpled and looks like it's had something on it that's been previously erased. Taking in all the information I was just given, and from what I have seen for myself, I can't help but worry about the boy haunting my dreams.

I wonder how much of what I was just told is true and what is just rumor. Either way, there are two things I know to be true. One, I want to know more about him. And two, he was right. My silly little bear seems pretty silly now.

Chapter Three

T he noise of the cafeteria is deafening as the chatter and continuous laughter creates a ringing in my ears. Sometimes... no more than sometimes I wish that I could escape somewhere quiet to eat. Just enjoy the silence and isolation. But I "must socialize" because "connections are everything." Blah, blah, blah.

"Over here!" Marryanne's hand shoots up, waving me over to the table where she, Christian, and a few others are already eating. I'm late to lunch, thanks to my meeting with the cheer coach to arrange our practice times.

Making my way over to their table, I smile and greet the other students who call my name.

The spaghetti served today is not a good combination with the white blouse I'm wearing, so I skip the stain waiting to happen and pick at my salad.

"How are your classes going, Millie?" Christian asks with a mouth full of noodles, and I cringe as I watch the sauce splatter all over the tray as he slurps them up.

"Uh. Fine. I guess. Nothing special really. Although I have Mr. Gibbins for math, so I'm a little worried. I heard he's pretty strict."

"Nah, you're pretty, so you'll be fine. He is only tough on the uglies."

"The uglies?" What does that even mean?

Christian is a year older than us, and he had Mr. Gibbins last year, so he has been beneficial in giving us all the details and tricks to passing each teacher.

"Yeah, the kids who are nerdy and strange. I think he wants them to 'rise to their potential.'" He drops his voice to mimic the grumpy old teacher, and we all giggle at his spot-on impersonation. "Just give minimal effort, and you'll be fine. If you're pretty or popular, which you are both, he just lets you skate by."

Marryanne says something to Christian, but I tune them all out as Henry catches my eye. I watch as he quietly picks up his tray and thanks the cafeteria servers. One of them even slips him an extra roll that he tucks into his pocket.

I want to know who his friends are, so I continue to watch him to see where he sits. Our school cafeteria is nothing but cliques. Like most schools I guess, people tend to stick to what and who makes them feel safe. Too afraid to branch out and challenge what makes them comfortable.

Although, who am I to talk? I'm the pot calling the kettle black.

He makes his way through the room. His head stays down, watching his feet but somehow still managing to avoid the tables and benches, the wandering students, and the few feet I see kick out in an attempt to trip him up, but as if it takes no effort at all, he avoids them all. He doesn't sit at a table but instead walks right out the front doors leading to the side exit of the building.

I get up in a rush, almost spilling my spaghetti on my shirt in the process, but I manage to fumble with my tray and books, balancing them all. "Hey, I... almost forgot that I needed... um, to... speak with Principal McGivens. See you guys after school."

I don't wait for their reaction. I just scurry over to the trash can, drop my tray off at the "dirties" counter, and hurry outside.

Rushing through the door, I expect to find him on the stone steps, but he isn't.

Where the heck did he go? Stepping down to the blacktop and taking in the surrounding area, I don't see him anywhere. Okay, he isn't a freaking ghost. Where could he have gone? My determination to find him far outweighs my logical brain as I walk farther from the school.

It's not until I reach the dumpsters about fifty yards from the school that I hear someone talking.

"It's okay. You need to eat if you're going to get better. Come on now."

I immediately recognize Henry's voice. The voice that has been replaying over and over again inside my dreams. Peering around the dumpster, I see him kneeling in front of an old milk crate.

My shoes crunch against the gravel as I step in closer, and I pinch my nostril shut at the putrid smell wafting off the dumpsters.

"Don't come closer. You'll scare her, and she won't eat."

I don't listen to him as I take another step, curious about who he is talking about.

Releasing my nose and breathing in through my mouth, I kneel beside him as his focus remains solely on the creature inside the crate. He is holding his hand down into the crate and a small bird is pecking at the roll from lunch.

"What are you doing?"

"Shh. Whisper. She's still scared." He still hasn't looked at me, and it's mildly annoying. Normally, I can't get people to stop staring at me, but the one boy I want to look at me acts as if I'm nothing.

"What are you doing?" I repeat, in a whisper this time.

"I found her this morning when I was eating breakfast. I think her wing is broken."

He sits back on his heels, leaving the bread inside, and then fills an old tin can with some water from his own bottle.

"And you're keeping her as a pet?"

Finally, he looks at me, and my heart practically melts. Those crystal-blue eyes and dark brown hair are so vividly captivating that I think I might just faint.

"No. Birds aren't meant for captivity. They are meant to fly, to be free. I'm just helping her. Then when she is strong enough again, she can fly away."

I look back at the bird and notice that one wing is hanging lower than the other, and she doesn't seem to be moving it. Not like she is the other one. She pecks at the roll, and every few pecks, she stops and looks at me. As if she's challenging me to try to take the roll from her.

I giggle at the audacity. I can't believe I'm being challenged by a tiny bird. "How did you find her?"

He bites into his apple, the juices running down his chin a little, and he wipes them away with the back of his hand. I notice the sheen on his lips and wonder if an apple tastes sweeter from another's lips.

"I wanted some peace and quiet, so I came out here to eat. She was hopping around, and I noticed she needed help." He shrugs like that is something everyone would notice and do. But no, I don't think anyone I know would show such kindness.

"How long do you think she will need until she is better?"

The ache in my legs begins to annoy me as I continue to hold the kneeling position, so I stand and brush down my skirt.

"Here." Henry lays his sweater out for me to sit on. It's just a lightweight knit since it's the beginning of September. But they keep the classroom freezing, so a sweater is a must for almost every student.

"Oh, that's okay. I don't want it to get dirty."

He raises a brow at me like the thought is amusing.

"Well. More dirty. I guess."

"It's just a sweater. Sit."

Well, if he insists. "Thank you," I say as I tuck my skirt in and sit with my legs tucked under me and off to the side. "A lady's posture" as my mother would say. She has a specific posture for every seating arrangement. In a chair, on the ground, in the car, on horseback. You name it, she has a proper way to sit.

"So? How long?"

"Hmm?" he says with a mouth full of apple.

"How long until she is better?"

He takes a piece from his mouth and puts it in the crate for the bird. She immediately begins pecking away at it. Such a trusting little thing.

"Oh. Uh. I don't know. Couple of days, maybe a week."

The silence carries between us as I think about the bird. About Henry and why he eats out here.

"Why are you out here anyway?" he asks as he takes a glass jar from his backpack and shovels the spaghetti into it.

I'm so distracted by what he is doing that I don't answer right away, and when he has packed up all of his lunch except the apple he ate, I finally return to my senses. "I followed you."

"Why?" The defensiveness in his tone makes me feel like I did something wrong when I know I didn't, and I don't like his attitude.

"Because I can. I don't see a sign saying 'no girls allowed' in your little dumpster club."

He scoffs like I'm silly. "Clearly, girls are allowed, or else little Pig wouldn't be here."

"Who?" I snark back. Did he just call me a pig?

He points at the bird, and I laugh, a little snort escaping. "You named the bird Pig?"

"It's an appropriate choice, given how much she eats."

"Okay, that's fair, I guess." My laughter dies out as I notice him looking at me. And the way he looks at me feels different from any other gaze. It feels like he is seeing my heart, not my name or clothes. As if I could be just like that bird and he would care for me, show me kindness when no one else would.

"I should call you pig."

My smile drops, and now I want to throw the closest hard object at him. "Excuse me?"

"When you laughed just now, you gave a cute little snort. Like a pig."

My jaw drops. How rude of him! God to think... Wait, did he say cute? Does he think I'm cute?

"I did not," I say with less force than I meant to because now all I can think about is him calling me cute. Or my laugh is cute. Whatever, same thing.

He doesn't respond, just continues to munch on his apple. Eating it down to the core, then eating the core. My nose wrinkles at the thought of eating an apple core but then I remember what Christian said about him and his family. How he packed the lunch probably to take home to help feed his brothers.

"I could give you my lunch tomorrow too, if you wanted to take it home for your brothers?"

His eyes shoot to mine, narrowed and glaring, and I notice a change in his posture, more tense and guarded now. "I don't need anything from you."

"I just want to help. You all need it more than I do. I can have my nanny pack me a lunch, and then you can have my school lunch. She won't mind. Really. Especially when I tell her why."

He laughs quietly to himself and shakes his head as he looks down at his lap. "Tell me, księżniczka, why is it that she won't mind?" His eyes meet mine again, and I want to crawl back inside myself with how burning they are. "Because you're doing a good deed for the poor boy at school? Is it so you can mark on your college application that you were charitable to the less fortunate?"

I'm stunned for a moment, the air in my lungs freezing until I'm finally able to find my courage again. "No... I just. I heard about you and your family, and I just want to help." Why is he being so mean about this? I'm offering him free food. I don't mean anything mean about it.

"And what did you hear about me?"

"I... Things." I don't want to bring up the loss of his mother or what people say about him. I know I wouldn't want people talking about me that way and now I realize I have myself in a bit of a pickle with this situation.

"Please elaborate. Because from my experience, most of what you hear about someone from someone else is hardly accurate. So if you're going to embarrass me with your charity, then please allow me to clarify any rumors about my family and me."

"I didn't mean to embarrass you, and it isn't charity," I bite back at him. The energy within myself is changing. Before, I felt bad that I had upset him. But now, well, now, he is just being a big jerk, and I don't deserve it.

He remains silent, challenging me with those blue eyes, and I challenge him right back. Standing and brushing my skirt off, I cross my arms and look down at him.

"I heard that your mom passed away and that it's just you, your dad, and your brothers. And clearly"—I look him up and down—"you don't have a lot of money. I didn't mean to offend. I was just trying to help, but if you're going to be a jerk about it, then I won't."

Turning on my heel, I sweep down and grab my bag off the floor, but a hand wraps around my wrist.

"Wait." His eyes are back to their calm blue. The blue that makes me feel seen.

"I'm sorry. Will you come back?"

The bell rings out, signaling the end of lunch. "Tomorrow. Come back?" he asks again.

"Only because I like Pig."

The corner of his lips turns up, and I find myself returning the smile before rushing off to class.

# Chapter Four

T he blur of the fair around me brings a smile to my lips. It's all so chaotic, wild, and... free. Everything I'm not. The lights that blink rapidly draw attention away from me. The screams of children and ringing of winning games drown out the never-ending checklist that runs through my head. The fair has always been my escape, where I go to blend in and hide. But for the first time, I find myself wanting to be found.

My mind drifts to Henry. I want him to find me, seek me out, talk to me. Is he behind the concessions again, shooting tin cans with his rubber band gun? Is he walking around, enjoying a funnel cake or playing games? Is he with his friends? A girl?

My chest aches at the thought of him with another girl. Why is it doing that?

The weeks have gone by fast, and soon, the fair will leave town, and I will find myself counting down the days until it returns. But I find I'm not as hopeless as I usually am because Henry makes me feel the way the fair does. Normal, free, a little wild.

Each day at lunch, we meet behind the dumpster, tending to Pig the bird. She is getting stronger. We had to get her a larger box so she could have more room to stretch her wings. Her once limp wing now settles naturally against her little body, and sometimes, she will stretch it out. But she still has yet to fly.

We leave the box open with no lid on top so that she can fly away when she is ready.

I begged Henry to cover her box so that a predator wouldn't attack her, but Henry just shrugged and told me that what's meant to be will be. If she is meant to fly, she will. If she is meant to die, she will.

I went home and cried.

But I didn't tell him that.

At first, I thought he was just being a typical boy about it. But then each day, she is there. And each day, I have a little more hope that she was meant to fly.

Christian's laughter pulls my thoughts from our little Pig, and I notice him tossing popcorn at Marryanne. She is trying to catch the pieces in her mouth as she sits atop the table, laughing more than anything.

"Come on, Miss Marry, it's not even that hard!" he teases.

"Oh well, why don't you try if it's so easy!"

Christian tosses a kernel of popcorn into the air and easily catches it in his mouth.

"Show off," Marryanne mumbles.

I sit at the table across from them, eating my funnel cake and looking around at all the lights... okay, looking for Henry. But I have yet to see him.

As Christian finishes off his bag of popcorn, he tosses the white-and-red-striped bag to the dirty ground and walks off, calling me to catch up.

Shaking my head, I bend down to pick up the bag, but a voice stops me. "I got it."

*Henry.*

Leaning up, he is already reaching down and putting the bag into a large tin can.

"You didn't have to." I bite at my bottom lip, suddenly feeling a bit shy around him for reasons I couldn't explain.

"It's my job. Literally."

I tilt my head at him, and he must read the confusion on my face.

"I work here. My title is 'Grounds Keeper,' but really, I'm just a glorified trash can." He walks over to another piece of trash and puts it into the can he is dragging behind him.

"Why do you work here?"

Now he looks at me like he is confused. "The same reason any other person works. I need the money."

"But why?"

He chuckles to himself. "Oh, księżniczka. What it would be like to be you."

I chase him, not letting him get away with what he is insinuating. "Hey, my life isn't all that it's cracked up to be, you know."

"Sure," he whispers without even looking at me.

"Really. I'm serious."

"Okay," he says. I should let him get back to work, but I don't want to. I like being around him.

"Well, what are you going to buy with your money? My daddy gives me an allowance each month as long as I keep my grades up. But I'm saving it up for something special. Are you saving for something?"

"Something special, huh?" The twinkle in his blue eyes sends butterflies erupting in my stomach. Oh goodness.

"Yeah. I'll tell you if you tell me what you are saving for?"

"Food," he says as he picks up a tin can and tucks it into a burlap sack tied to his belt.

His one-word reply makes me stop in my tracks. Food. The money isn't for him.

God, I feel so stupid. Here I am, saving my money for a pair of white leather Mary Janes with sparkles, and his family can barely afford to eat.

"So what are you saving for?" He continues the conversation nonchalantly like he didn't just flip my entire perspective. I knew his family wasn't well off, but I never considered that any family didn't have the means to do something as simple and necessary as eating.

I should have known. The way he eats only a few bites of his lunch each day and packs the rest away. The way he defensively denied my help to bring him food. He was embarrassed. Or maybe ashamed?

"I, uh... It's nothing." Tucking my hair behind my ear, suddenly feeling very childish, I try to walk past him, but he grabs my hand and turns me toward him again.

"Tell me."

"No. Really. It's silly."

"But it matters to you, right? Like the bear?"

I reach down to my feet, picking up a can and placing it in his sack. "It's a pair of sparkly Mary Janes." I don't look at him as I say it. I can't. I don't want to see the look on his face, but in my attempt to avoid his eyes, I see his shoes. With the holes, the dirt, the broken soles.

God, I am so selfish. I have ten pairs of shoes in my closet right now, and he doesn't even have a single pair that is proper and put together.

A sudden rush of guilt and shame fills me, and tears spring from my eyes as a sob breaks through my lips. "I'm so sorry. Shoes are so silly."

I cover my face with my hands, but I feel him wrap his own around my wrists and pull them away. My eyes meet his, and I drown in his gentle eyes.

"Then why are you crying over them? They're just shoes."

The way he says it makes me feel like he isn't talking about my Mary Janes but his own tattered ones.

"Come on." He pulls me away from the moment in a rush, and I eagerly follow. I don't know where he is taking me, but it doesn't matter. I'd go anywhere with him.

"Where are we going?" I shout out as he rushes off, dragging me behind him.

He finally comes to a stop behind the concessions counter where we first met and holds up a wooden slingshot with a worn rubber band.

"Here."

My eyes glare holes into the wood. What does he expect me to do with that?

"Come on, take it."

I wipe the tears that have leaked from my eyes and spilled onto my cheeks and grab the warm wood handle. "I don't know what to do with this."

"Let me show you." He steps behind me and turns us to face the log, then runs out from behind me and pulls some tins from the sack at his hip. Lining them up, he adjusts them so they are all straight, then runs back to me.

His warm body stands behind me, so close that I can feel his breath on my cheek. "Okay, so just grab a small rock, small enough to fit into this piece here." He tugs on the small piece of fabric wrapped around the rubber band. The fabric is frayed at the edges from use, and I wonder how many times he has shot from this old toy. "Then just pull back, aim, and release."

"Like a bow and arrow?"

"Yeah. Kinda."

I do as he says, leaning down to find a rock, then notching it in the rubber band. I aim, and his breath tickles me again as my rock flies to some unknown location. A ping sounds off the tin roof of the concessions stand.

"Oh my God!" I half laugh and half shriek. What if I hit some-one!? This weapon should not be in my hands.

Henry's laughter is one of the most beautiful sounds I have ever heard. I'm mesmerized by him. How strange it is that someone with absolutely nothing has the most carefree and joyous laugh. As if that's all he needs in his life to be happy.

"That was awful!" He doubles over, clutching his stomach. Still laughing.

"Hey, you jerk! It's harder than it looks!" I pick up another rock and sling it at him. It hits him in the side as he turns to try to avoid the attack.

"Oh, you're in for it now, księżniczka."

I see the look in his eyes and immediately regret my choice. Taking off, I bolt for the grass field behind us and hear his footsteps take chase.

A laugh bursts from my chest as I feel him at my back, then he tackles me to the soft ground. He rolls us so I am lying atop him, his heavy breaths making our chests move in sync. I try desperately to wiggle free even though I want nothing more than to stay here in his arms forever.

"Oh no, you don't. Come back, księżniczka."

His hands dig into my sides, and I let out a snort as my body shakes while he tickles me.

"Not the snort!" he yells.

"Stop!" I laugh, but it only encourages him more as he continues his assault.

We stay there, laughing and smiling in what feels like a suspended reality. He is everything. Everything I want. Everything I want to be.

As our laughter dies and our breathing settles, we fall into a peaceful silence as we gaze at each other. His blue eyes match my own, but they have seen a completely different world. But I see him. I recognize the goodness in him. The resilience despite his reality.

His finger comes up, brushing my cheek, and I feel the swipe of dirt stain my skin. The grittiness of the mud beneath us painted on like rouge.

"There. Now you're real," he whispers, and I fall.

## Chapter Five

"Mills, why don't you go eat with your friends today?" His eyes beg me. But that's all the more suspicious because Henry never begs.

It's been a month since he tackled me in the grass field, and I fell in love with him. A month we have been eating together each day. A month and he has yet to kiss me.

I tell my friends I'm off working with a tutor at lunch. A part of me is afraid of what they will think if I admit I'm spending my time with Henry. And the guilt of that eats at me. I shouldn't care, but I was raised to believe that image is everything. And that's hard to let go of.

What will people see me as if I'm not what they need me to be?

A bigger part, however, wants to protect what Henry and I have, and I know when people find out, they will talk, and our little world will cease to exist.

But lunch is our time. Why would he want me to go with my friends all of a sudden?

"No. I want to eat with you and Pig. I brought her strawberries today. They are her favorite." I push past him.

"Mills, no!" He reaches out to me, but he isn't quick enough, and I see her. My little Pig lying in her crate.

Dead.

*If she was meant to fly, she will. If she was meant to die, she will.*

I crouch down and scoop her up into my hands. "No. No. No."

"I'm so sorry, księżniczka," Henry consoles as he leans down and cups his hands around mine.

"But she was doing so well. She was healing. I thought..." I feel foolish to admit my hope for her.

"She wasn't meant to fly, Mills."

"She was!" I stand abruptly, clutching her to my chest. "She was meant to fly! I took care of her! I... she was better! She can't die!"

My tears flow faster than Henry can wipe them away. His rough, stained fingers smudge the rouge on my cheeks as it mixes with my tears.

"Shhh." Wrapping me into his arms, he brings my head to his shoulder and tries to soothe me. I don't know why I'm reacting this way.

Pig was just a bird.

But she was my bird. Our bird.

"Do you want to help me bury her?" Henry asks as I sniffle into his shoulder. The smell of oil and firewood clings to him, and it has become one of my favorite scents. It almost immediately calms me.

"Yes. Can we bury her in the field?"

"Sure. Come on."

I know I should wait until after school. If we leave now, we won't make it back in time for sixth period, but I just don't care. At this moment, I don't care if people know I skipped class. I don't care if they see me with Henry because right now, he, and he alone, is all I want.

He takes Pig from my hands and wraps her in a handkerchief, then puts her in his backpack for the mile walk to the now empty field where the fair was held.

The idea of the fair reminds me that he no longer has any way to bring in money. "Now that the fair is gone, what will you do for money?" I ask as I grab my backpack and wipe the remaining tears from my face with the back of my sweater sleeve.

He shrugs. "I'll figure it out."

We walk until we are off school grounds, and the busy streets of cars honking and people milling about fill the silence.

"I could help, you know. I have some extra—"

"Stop, księżniczka. I don't want your money."

"But I want to help." I watch my feet, feeling both sadness and anger at him. Why must he be so stubborn? Why can't he accept the help I'm offering? I could give him enough each week to feed his dad and brothers. They wouldn't have to worry.

"You do help, Mills."

"How?"

"Henry?" A large man with kind eyes and dark hair comes up to us.

"Tato? Did you get off early?"

And although I don't know what Tato means, it's not hard to tell this is Henry's father. They are almost identical. "Boss needed me to run an errand for him. Why aren't you in school?"

My father would be furious if he found me skipping school, but this man looks concerned.

"Uh..." He looks at me, then back at his father. "This is Millie. She is a friend."

Okay. Ouch...

"Her bird died—"

"Our bird." I interrupt as I cross my arms over my chest and pout. First, he calls me a friend, and then he is going to try to deny that Pig wasn't his also. She was *ours*.

"*Our* bird died, and we wanted to bury her. Millie is really upset about it." He nudges my side with his elbow, cuing me to put on the waterworks.

I relax the scowl and put on my biggest puppy dog eyes. Batting my lashes up at Henry's father, I pout out my lip and sniffle a bit. "She meant the world to me, Mr...uh—"

"Call me Alek."

"Mr. Alek, I loved her so much, and I couldn't spend the whole day in class knowing she was just sitting out behind the dumpster...dead." I tack on the last word, hoping to get a little extra pity.

Henry snorts, then bursts into laughter at my side. "God, that was good. You should be an actress, księżniczka."

"I hope you're kidding, son. That was the poorest performance I ever saw."

My tears dry just as quickly as they came, and the scowl returns to my face. "What is going on here?" I stomp my foot and fist my hands at my sides. "Are you making fun of me?"

"No. No. I would never, księżniczka. I just... didn't think you would put so much effort into the act. And it was a great act. Really." He tries and fails to hold back his laughter as his hand tries to grasp onto mine, but I bat it away as I cross my arms over my chest.

"Go bury your bird, then get back to school, you two." Alek chuckles, then ruffles Henry's hair and continues down the street.

I stare at his back as he walks away. I'm amazed that he let us go that easily and furious that he played into all this.

"I really dislike you right now," I mumble as I walk off, not even waiting for Henry. He can tail after me if he wants to apologize. I'm making him work for my forgiveness.

"Aw, come on, Mills. That was funny." Wrapping his arms around my waist from behind, he stops me, and I feel my anger melting away. "I'm sorry." He places a soft kiss to my cheek, and my butterflies take flight.

"Pig's passing is nothing to be joked about," I remind him, still refusing to look at him even though he was already forgiven as soon as that beautiful laugh erupted from his chest.

"You're right, księżniczka. I'm really, really sorry." He moves his head to the other side and places a kiss on that cheek now.

"Should I get down on my knees and beg?" I hear the smile in his voice. I fight... and fail to hold in my own smile.

"Stop. You're being ridiculous. I'll need flowers. Lilies are my favorite. Dinner... and a movie. Then I'll think about forgiving you."

"Done. Just give me time."

My smile drops. Right. Time to save. I immediately regret my words. Shoot. Why don't I think about this kind of stuff before I speak? God, I'm an idiot. I've never had to be mindful like this before.

Turning in his arms, I take in his handsome face. So young but I know behind the youth is a grown man... grown because he had to be.

"No. I don't want that. I shouldn't have said that..."

His brows furrow, and his jaw clenches. "Do you not think I can give you that? Because I can."

"Henry..." I plead. Please don't make me say it.

"What?" He's angry now. Dang. I can't do anything right with him. I'm so out of my normal.

"You... You shouldn't spend money on me like that. You need that money for food, clothes—"

He steps back, the loss of his body connecting with mine impacting me more than I expected.

"Forget it," he says with his back to me as he continues his walk to the field.

I chase him, not ignorant to the fact that it's now me who needs forgiveness. "Henry, please stop." I reach out and grab his elbow, his jacket coarse in my hands and reminding me of the condition his clothes are in. "Talk to me."

He jerks his elbow from my hand. "If you don't think I can give you what you want 'cause I'm the slum, the dirty kid, the lowest of low, then why are you here? Huh?"

"Don't do this. You know I don't care about those things."

With the pace he's moving, we're almost to the field now, but he spins around, and I almost crash into him. I swallow hard, not sure what to expect.

"Then why do you ignore me in the hallways? Why don't you talk to me when you're walking with your friends down the street? You glance at me with those pretty blue eyes but nothing more. Are you ashamed of me?"

I'm silent because he is right. I do all of those things, and I didn't think he noticed. I thought that since he had always been the quiet kid, the one people ignored, he also ignored everything around him. But I should have known better. Henry notices all the little details.

"I would understand, you know. You're you. Perfect. Beautiful. Delicate. The mayor's daughter. You're everything and have everything. What do I have to offer you?"

"Henry." It's a whisper I didn't even mean to say out loud. I reach up and brush the hair from his eyes. His locks are longer than the other boys wear theirs, a little greasy and messy because I know that how he looks is the least of his worries. But I love them. I love the way his wavy hair hangs over his forehead, and the way he shakes his head to clear his eyes when a particular piece is being unruly.

"I don't have everything. I don't have you."

I don't want him thinking this way. Thinking about himself that way or about how he thinks I see him or about what he thinks I want. He never cared before. In the past month, he has never cared about what he couldn't give me. He just wanted to be with me.

He's letting those thoughts get into his head. I'm letting them get into his head through my own foolish actions. I need him to come back to me.

"Please believe me."

His eyes glance at my lips, and I would sell my soul for just a single kiss.

*Please, kiss me.*

"Let's put Pig to rest."

He turns away from me, and I'm left feeling like I ruined everything.

# Chapter Six

The locker slamming at my side jolts me from my daydream. Said daydream is leaning up against the lockers across from me, reading out of his science textbook. His foot is cocked up, resting against the lockers, and his calm, cool demeanor makes me wonder how no one has noticed how handsome he is before.

His dark hair and light eyes are stunning. His high cheekbones and full lips make me want to die. He is a walking dream, and now I'm happy that I'm the only one who has noticed. Once girls look past the dirty, tattered clothes and shy attitude, they would be all over him. I do not like that idea.

"Who are you looking at like that?" Marryanne says flirtatiously as she follows my gaze.

"Wait... Not that Henry kid? You're not serious?"

"What? He's handsome, and he is actually really nice."

Clutching her books to her chest, she turns to look at him and tilts her head. Assessing him.

I don't like it.

I don't like her looking at him.

I don't like her judging him.

"I mean, I guess there is potential if he wasn't so... dirty. I mean look at his shoes. They have holes in them."

"They're just shoes, Marryanne." I roll my eyes and close my own locker after collecting the books I need.

"Doesn't matter. Also, he should take a bath. He smells like those men who work in the mines."

"Be nice," I warn. But I'm not brave enough to put too much bite into it.

"Whatever." She links her arm with mine and pulls me toward our homeroom class.

Looking back at Henry, I find his eyes are already locked on me. I smile at him and follow his eyes as he looks down at his shoes and wiggles his toes... which I can see through the holes, and when I look back up to his eyes, he smirks and winks at me.

At lunch, I meet Henry in the library. The chilly weather keeps us indoors now, so the library is where we find solace.

"Could you tell me about your brothers?"

"What do you want to know?" he says with a mouth full of turkey sandwich.

"Maybe their names? A little about them? Do you actually have eleven of them?"

He chuckles at that, finishes his bite and takes a drink of water, then turns fully toward me.

"Yeah. I do. Antoni, Alfred, Michal, Niko, Tomasz, Jakub, Jan, Elijah, Markus, Peter, and Marcel." He counts each name on a finger, then has to start over for the eleventh brother. Each name he says with a bit of an accent, which I would assume is Polish since that's where I heard his parents are from.

"And you all are from Poland?"

"My parents are. Then Antoni, Alfred, Michael, and Niko were all born there. The rest of us were born here. Antoni and Alfred are twins. As well as Jakub and Jan."

"And where are you in the mix?"

"I'm the youngest. But not the smallest," he says with a flirtatious glint in his eye and a snarky little grin.

A blush creeps up my neck, but I keep the conversation moving. "And your mom and dad?"

"Mama died giving birth to me. After having so many children... her body just couldn't do it. I've been told I almost died also. My dad was able to save me but not Mama."

He takes another bite, and I realize I've been so invested in what he has been saying that I have forgotten to eat, so I take my first bite. He talks as if this is all so normal. Having so many siblings, having lost his mom... how does he really feel behind the mask he's wearing?

Then it hits me... his dad? "Wait, your dad delivered you?"

The muscles of his jaw flex as he chews. "Yup. He delivered all of us."

"She didn't go to the hospital?"

"Couldn't afford it. It's common where I come from for babies to be delivered in the homes."

Oh my God. Would they have been able to save his mom if they could have afforded a hospital? I can't let that thought run through my head, but how could I not? Does he wonder that as well?

Brushing a piece of my hair out of my face, he gives me a reassuring smile. "Mills, not even a doctor could have saved her."

His ability to read me is somewhat terrifying but also incredibly soothing. I never need to hide with him, as if I could.

"Where are your older brothers?"

He grabs my hand and lifts it as if inspecting it, then begins running his fingers up and down my own. One by one, he traces the outside of my fingers. Then he lets our hands fall, but he doesn't let go as he strokes my thumbnail with his own repeatedly.

"Antoni and Alfred work in a factory near the city. They send us money when they can. Michal, Niko, Thomaz, Jakub, and Jan work in the mines with Tato, while Elijah and Markus and I go to school."

"Yes, I've seen them around. One is a senior, and one is a junior, right?"

He nods.

"When did the others graduate?"

"They didn't," he says as if it was obvious.

"What do you mean? They didn't go to school?"

He pulls his eyes from our hands and looks at me. I can see the pain in his eyes. The guilt. "Some of us are meant to fly...We all make sacrifices to survive, księżniczka. Some of us had to give up more than the others."

"That's so sad."

"Don't be sad for us. We're happy."

"How?" I say it before I can stop myself. My filter takes the backburner like it often does, and I cringe a tad, but Henry doesn't seem to take offense. He smiles as if recalling a memory. "We just are. We all have our roles, and we have each other."

"You're never alone."

"Never. And neither are you. Not anymore."

"It's funny how I have all this stuff, but it means nothing. There is no weight to it. It could all just fly away at the whisper of the wind."

He doesn't reply with his words. Only the soft traces of his fingers serve as a reminder that he is still here, listening. It all seems so pointless. The friends I have only like me because of the connections I can offer them, the clothes I wear, and the social status I bring them because I'm the mayor's daughter. If I were a nobody, nothing, they wouldn't give me a second glance. Just like they do Henry.

He may not have the money, the shoes, the car, hell, even the food that we do, but he is rooted in his family. He's happy with what he has.

"Mills?" He brushes his fingers across my cheek. "The bell."

I come out of my mind, back to him and realize I was so lost in my own thoughts of how lonely and superficial my life is that I didn't even realize the bell had rung.

His lips brush my forehead as he stands and begins toward the door. "Can I see you after school?"

"I'm working, księżniczka. But I'll see you tomorrow. Same place."

His absence sits heavy on me. Everything is lighter when he is near. I can't imagine going any length of time without him. It would kill me.

*Come back to me.*

*I don't want to go out there.*
*It's all so lonely without you.*

Chapter Seven

As the end of November approaches, I feel myself rooting deeper and deeper into Henry. He has become the only real thing in my life. The only thing I find myself caring for.

Mom and Dad are as absent as they usually are and even more so around the holidays. I'm not sure what it is about the holidays that make people want to hold more benefits and galas, but they "must attend for appearance's sake" as Daddy says. And of course, they never take me like they said they one day would.

Mrs. Evelyn has been doting on me, buying me new dresses and shoes and ribbons, but it's all just filler. I can see the hurt in her eyes as she does her best to fill my parents' void. It's not her fault they're absent, and she does what she can.

But only one person has been able to make me feel special.

My Henry.

Christian and Marryanne invited me to a movie tonight, and I decided to join. Henry can never meet up in the evenings since he works, and I didn't feel like being stuck at home alone on a Friday night. So being with them is better than by myself, right?

As we exit the theater after the movie, Marryanne plugs her nose and grimaces. "Oh my God. What is that smell? Oh, wait. It's just Henry."

"What?" I look around and spot him sweeping up outside the theater.

"Looks like the trash is hanging with the trash. Some things never change." Christian chuckles as Marryanne laughs as well.

"Stop that. You don't even know him," I defend as a fire rises in my chest. God, why are they so awful to someone who hasn't done anything to them?

"Oh, come on, Millie, we're just having some fun." Christian tosses his popcorn box at Henry, and it lands right in front of him. "Oops. Missed the trash can."

"But, Christian, there isn't even a trash can over there. Oh, you meant poor Henry? I mean, he smells and looks like one. I can see the confusion." They both laugh, and my fists clench at my sides.

Henry looks at me and shakes his head as he leans down and picks up the box and walks five feet from us to throw it away.

"Mills," he says as he looks at me with hope in his eyes. Hope for what? That I'll stand up for him. Be brave enough to set myself apart?

"Don't tell me you two actually know each other?" Christian's laughter dies down a bit. "Oh, come on, man... wait, did you think you could get a girl like my Millie here? Do you own a mirror? Or soap, for that matter?" He slings his arm over my shoulders, and I find myself vibrating with anger at the horrible things he is saying.

"Stop it, Christian," I growl through my teeth.

"I think I saw some spilled pop on aisle C. Might want to get on that, trash boy."

"That's it." I push Christian off me and stomp toward Henry.

I'm so sick and tired of them treating Henry like that, and I'm even more sick and tired of hiding behind them, doing nothing to help and everything to feed into the cruel things they say about the boy who is kind but different.

"Henry," I say, and he turns, surprise written all over his face.

I don't think.

I just act.

Taking his face in my hands, I slam my lips to his and taste the sweet flavor of honey and butter on his lips. I don't take the moment to savor him beyond that. I pull back when he doesn't return my kiss. I feel like maybe I misread everything because his eyes are blown wide, and surprise is written all over him.

"What the fu—" I hear Christian say, but I don't hear the rest as Henry drops his broom and wraps his hands around my waist, pulling me in. He seals his lips with mine once again, and I know I just sealed my fate.

A fate I can live with as long as Henry is mine.

The world slows to a halt, and the noises in my head quiet as his lips brush mine. His tongue asks for more as he brushes it against my lips, and I give him everything. He pulls away, panting heavily, and leans his forehead against mine. "What was that?"

"I'm sorry for how they treat you."

"Was that a pity kiss?" he whispers.

"It's just a kiss."

"My first kiss will never be just a kiss because it was with you."

His first kiss... was with me?

"I'm off in fifteen minutes. Wait for me?" His fingers brush my hair behind my ears as he pulls back to look into my eyes. I see it as much as I feel it. That kiss broke something in each of us. Something that was holding us back. And I can't wait to see where we go from here.

"I'll be here."

I turn away from him, our hands lingering, clinging to each other like they don't want to let go. But they finally come apart, and I turn with a silly smile on my face to my friends.

"What the hell, Millie?" Christian says, anger infiltrating his tone.

"What? Henry is a good guy, way better than the lot of you. He cares for me, not for who my family is, and if you can't accept him, then you can drop me."

Marryanne comes up next to me. "Honey, you think we care about you just 'cause of your money? We have our own... but what do you think he's really after?" She tilts her head and gives me a look that says I'm as dumb as a box of rocks, but I know she's wrong. I'm the one who chased him out to the dumpster that day.

"You're wrong. About him and about me. I'll see you guys at school on Monday." With that, I turn away and go to wait in the little café next to the theater.

I can't believe I did that. I mean, it was long overdue, and I thought he would be the one to initiate our first kiss, but maybe he was nervous since it was his first kiss. Either way, I'm not sorry I did it. In fact, I can't get the butterflies to settle down inside my stomach. They are flitting about having a blast in there, and I'm not complaining. He's the only one who has and ever will make me feel this way.

After fifteen minutes, I head back to the theater and find him waiting for me at the doors. He takes my hand and drags me to one of the theaters. The large space feels even bigger when it's empty.

"What are we doing?" I giggle as he hauls me up the steps, and we settle into the empty seats at the back.

"Anything you want."

Anything I want? All I can think about is one thing. One thing I want to do over and over and over again. "I want to kiss you."

"Then kiss me, księżniczka."

## Chapter Eight

I was right. That kiss... and the many that followed changed everything. Something drastically shifted inside my mind. I couldn't care less what anyone thought of me now that I had Henry. Looking back, I think I was keeping my friends close by as I explored my relationship with Henry. Just in case he wasn't what I thought, and he broke my heart. But once I knew he was mine, when he took me in his arms and kissed me like I owned him, I had the confidence to shed my superficial life.

Over the past two months, Henry and I have been inseparable at school. I'm with him at any free moment, which has been few between cheer and student council and him working extra hours lately. I didn't win the class president position, but I'm honestly not disappointed. I never wanted that position, and I realized I was only doing it to be noticed by my father and accepted by my mother.

Cheer has also been something I've let go of. I gave the captain position to Marryanne since it meant more to her anyway. Mama was not happy about that, but I'm living for me now. Not them.

I also told my parents I didn't want to go to an Ivy League. They still don't accept women, but Mama and Daddy believe they will by the time I go to college. I told them that I wasn't sure what I wanted to do. Maybe be a teacher? Maybe a nurse? I don't know, but I'm also only fourteen. Why do I have to have it all figured out right now?

Right now, all I want is to be in love.

Henry has been teaching me a little Polish and telling me about his family. The foods that his mom used to make and the songs she would sing that have now been passed down to his brothers. I don't recognize any of the words, but I find myself humming the melodies. He says that he feels like she's always with him through his family and the pieces of her they each carry. I can't imagine how he must feel being the only one who doesn't remember her, well, him and Marcel, as Marcel was only a little over a year old when she died.

He finally told me what księżniczka means. He had some groveling to do after that. All this time, he has been calling me princess. I'm not a princess.

"Hi, księżniczka." Henry comes up behind me in the lunch line and whispers in my ear, "I have a surprise for you."

But he isn't holding anything. Or wearing anything different. Nothing seems to be out of the ordinary.

My brow raises in question as I try to figure out what it could be. "Well? What is it?" I prod at him.

He tsks at me as he waves his finger back and forth in front of my face, and I smack it away. "It wouldn't be a surprise if I told you. Can you meet me at the diner tonight at seven?"

Narrowing my eyes, I try with all I have to read him, but he's not giving me anything. Just that cute little smirk.

"I'll be there."

"Good. Wear something nice."

I tilt my head at him, thoroughly confused now. He's never asked me to dress up, but I'll comply.

Before I can interrogate him, he rushes off, leaving a quick kiss to my cheek. I notice the glances we get, like the ones aimed at me now. Some are disgusted, some confused. But I don't care about any of them.

The day drags on as the anticipation for tonight eats at my mind. What could he have for me? What has he done?

When the time finally comes, I hop out of the car as I wave to Mrs. Evelyn. I picked out a blue dress, the same color as Henry's eyes, and paired it with brown leather Mary Janes. A white ribbon holds back half of my blonde hair, which I asked Mrs. Evelyn to help me curl.

I wanted to look nice but not over the top so I hope this will do.

As I turn from the car after shutting the door, I see Henry.

He stands in black high-waisted dress slacks. The waistband is scrunched by the belt he has holding them up. Clearly, they are too big for him, but they are... clean. Crisp lines and no stains or tears. He has a white button-up shirt and dark blue tie. It's also too long for his torso, so it doesn't hit where it should. It's probably his dad's, based on how long it is. His shoes are the same ones he wears each day but now have leather patches sewn over the toes.

As he sees me, he pulls out a bouquet of lilies from behind his back. The vibrant white shines in the dark night.

"Henry."

"I can't do much, Mills. Other guys, they could give you so much more. But I can lo—I can make you happy."

Tears fill my eyes and threaten to ruin the makeup I delicately applied, but it doesn't matter.

He holds out two tickets to the movies. I see they are for the cheapest seats offered, but it doesn't matter. I know how much he spent on these. Money that my father makes in two minutes of work, Henry would have to save months for.

And he did it. For me.

I lean in but feel something solid in the front pocket of his slacks. Looking down, he follows my gaze and pulls out a silver pocket watch with engraved filigree and an inscription along the edge. Much nicer than anything I have seen on him before.

"What is that?" I reach out and run my fingers over the edge, feeling the grooves and the engravings.

"My mother gave it to my father on their wedding day. It's all he has of hers anymore. All any of us have of her. But... Tato said that if I was to dress like a man tonight, no suit is complete without a nice watch. So he let me borrow it."

"It's beautiful." I notice an engraving around the watch face and lean in to read it. Not even knowing how to pronounce the words.

"Wiatr pod moimi skrzydłami," he says quietly.

"What does it mean?"

He grabs my hand in his and kisses my knuckles. "Wind beneath my wings."

Tipping up on my toes, I kiss his lips and repeat what he said to me in Polish. Absolutely failing at the easy way he says it. But he smiles anyway.

"Are you ready to go on our first date, księżniczka?"

"Take me away, Henry."

After the movie, I'm full of overwhelming glee. Nothing could have been better than this date. My favorite flowers, dinner at the diner, and then a movie to finish it. It has been more than anyone has ever done for me, and it means even more coming from Henry.

As Henry walks me home, I get a strange feeling. Something doesn't feel right and as I turn to look behind me, I see a man come up behind us fast. His face is covered, and he is holding something in his pocket.

"Henry!" I shout as the man grabs me from behind and pulls me to his chest.

Henry reaches out for me, but the man holds something cold and hard to my head. "Don't move, or I put a bullet in her brain."

"Please. Let her go," Henry pleads as he reaches a hand out to me, but his movements are careful.

"Empty your pockets. I want all you got, boy." The rumble of the man's chest pressed to my back forces a sob from my throat.

Henry reaches into his pockets but pulls them out empty. "Please, sir. I have nothing. Please—just let her go. I... I have... nothing." I can hear his voice break. The realization hits that he truly has nothing to offer in exchange for me. "You can take me. Take me and let her go."

"Why would I take you if you have nothing? Your fancy suit, you leaving the movies. You have to have something. Don't lie to me!"

The tip of what I know is a gun digs into my temple. Oh God. He's going to kill me. Henry's eyes search mine for forgiveness because he knows as well as I do, he can't protect me.

"I-I'm nobody. Please, you..." He pauses. Then reaches for the front pocket again, unclasping his father's watch from his belt.

"No, Henry." I whimper as the man's arm squeezes my throat tighter.

"My watch. Take my watch. I don't know how much it's worth, but it's gotta be worth something. Please, it's truly all I have. Let her go."

I see Henry begging the man with his eyes, but I can't tell what the man is doing. Moments pass. Is he considering taking the watch? What if he doesn't? What if he does?

I shake my head, but I don't know why. I don't know what I'm asking for, what I'm saying no to. Him giving up his father's watch for me or the fact that I don't want to die. I wasn't meant to die, not this early. I haven't had the chance to fly yet.

"The watch for the girl. I toss her; you toss the watch. At the same time."

Henry nods his head. "Okay. Just don't hurt her."

"One. Two. Three." He pushes me to the ground, my knees scrape against the gravel, ripping my tights, and my palms bleed from getting cut on a rock or piece of glass, I'm not sure which.

I hear the man running off, and then Henry is next to me, pulling me into his arms.

"Are you okay?" His fingers find the bottom of my chin, and he lifts my face to his. "Mills, look at me. Tell me you're okay?"

"I'm okay. But your father's watch... Henry."

"It's okay. It's just a watch." He holds me in silence for a few moments as both of us play over what just happened. "Let's get you home, okay?"

He helps me to my feet, and I look down, taking in the distress of my once perfect outfit. "I don't want to go home yet. Can we... I don't know. Do something else?"

He sighs out laughing. "You want to go do something else after that? Are you crazy?"

"Yeah." I look across from the alleyway we had been forced into and see a small coffee shop that still appears to be open. "There."

"Coffee? You want coffee at ten at night?"

I nod. I don't actually want coffee. I just don't want to be away from Henry, and I know that if I go home, he'll have to go home too.

We step into the shop, and the older lady at the counter takes us in. Our appearances must tell one heck of a story because she immediately pulls out two mugs and fills them with coffee. She adds a splash of cream into each and then pushes them toward us as we sit down at the counter. "On the house." She nods, then walks away.

I take the warm mug in my hand and let out a small laugh. "I've never actually had coffee before."

"Me either." He chuckles. "Together?"

I nod, and we both stare at each other as we take our first sip.

"Oh my God," I say.

"It's delicious," he moans.

"I could spend my whole life drinking this stuff." I take another sip, closing my eyes as I take in the soothing warmth, the rich flavor of the coffee, and the silkiness of the cream.

"I can see it now, Mill's Coffee House."

Chapter Nine

The walk from the coffee shop to my house is a short one. And I wish more than anything it was longer. I'm not ready to face the consequences of my actions. Staying out later than I had told Mrs. Evelyn I would be, and even worse, coming home with ripped tights and a dirty dress.

I stop Henry at the end of our white gravel driveway. Our front porch steps are about 100 yards away. The trees that line the long, straight road whisper to us in their own foreign language. My old, wise, sometimes a little cuckoo nanny once told me that the trees speak to one another, telling tales and warning us of dangers. But we have become disconnected from nature to the point that we can no longer understand them.

I wonder what they're saying now.

"Thank you for tonight, Henry. It's the first date I have ever been on, and it was perfect."

Our linked hands sway as we walk, and I feel him squeeze a bit tighter.

"I think our definitions of perfect are vastly different. I'm so sorry for what happened tonight. I—"

I stop him by giving a tug to his hand and move it so he's cradling my face. "Stop. We are okay. It's me who should be sorry. You had to give up your father's watch."

He lets out a breath and shakes his head, looking at our feet. "It's just a watch."

We continue to walk, this chilly air creeping in to caress my legs through the holes in my tights. "Despite what happened, I want you to know I loved our date. I want to plan our next one. Will you let me?"

"My manly ego may take a hit, but if that's what you want, I will comply with minimal complaints." He smiles down at me, and I return it. The weight of what happened tonight and what momentarily crept in a moment ago is gone. But that's how this young fourteen-year-old boy is. He has a way of letting go and focusing on what truly matters. I know inside he feels guilty, and he may even feel that for a while, but he doesn't let it change him. He doesn't hold on to it.

He walks me to the bottom of my front porch steps and brushes my hair from my face as I take in his beautiful glacial eyes. "I love your eyes," I whisper as I find myself getting lost in them.

"I love you."

My breath catches in my chest. Did he just...?

My heart pounds a mile a minute. "Are you sure?" My voice wavers as I try to hide my fear that his words don't mean what I want them to. He has to mean it. Because if he doesn't, I will not survive him leaving me behind.

"You are the wind beneath my wings, księżniczka." His forehead meets mine, our noses brushing.

"I love you too."

He seals his lips to mine, and I cling to him, silently begging him to never let me go, to never leave me, because I won't survive life without him. Call me silly or dumb, but even at fourteen, that Henry is mine forever.

The trees whisper. A warning.

"Get your dirty hands off my daughter." My father's voice booms out from the porch, and I jump back from Henry. He takes a moment to look at me, hurt written all over his features. Then he turns fully to face my father.

"Daddy. You're home?"

"We came back earl—" His eyes look up and down my tattered clothes, and his brows furrow. His gaze turns dangerously angry, and I can see the assumptions forming in his mind.

"Daddy, no. It's not what it looks like." He storms toward us and pulls me behind him.

"It looks like your clothes are ripped, and his hands and lips were just all over you. You're a child, Millie." His glare turns from me to Henry now. "Are you trying to trick her? Take something that isn't yours, boy?"

"Daddy, stop. This man attacked us, but I'm okay. Henry—" I tug at his arm to take a step back, but he doesn't budge.

"Hush, Millie. He is no good for you. It doesn't matter what he has or hasn't done." My father's eyes wander up and down Henry's frame, assessing, judging, criticizing. "What matters is the crowd he attracts, the danger that surrounds him. I will not allow you to be collateral damage to the life he will always live."

Henry stands still with this hands tucked into his pockets. He has no fear in his posture, just nonchalance that I know will aggravate my father more. "You're right, sir. Mills is too good for me, and she will just be collateral damage. I will never be able to offer her the life she deserves."

But... Please let there be a but.

But he doesn't continue.

"No, Henry. Daddy! Let me go."

My father turns toward me, concern in his eyes. I know what he does and says stems from a place of love, but he's wrong. He believes money and status matter more than love and happiness, and maybe before Henry, I would have agreed, but not anymore. He doesn't see Henry's heart like I do. He doesn't understand that the heart can offer more than any wallet ever could.

"You will not see him again, Millie. He will never be able to keep you safe. Look at you. You were clearly hurt, and he did nothing to stop it."

"You don't get to decide that! This is my life." I stomp my foot and try to wiggle away; all I want is to be in Henry's arms. I'm safe there. I'm accepted there. I'm *loved* there.

"It's okay, księżniczka. Your father loves you, and he is right. I can't protect you." His voice isn't angry or sad. It's just...numb, like he's already accepted what my father is saying and written it off as our future, but I won't allow that.

My mom rushes out now, hearing the commotion. "What in heavens is going on out here." Mama now looks me up and down. Her mask has slipped, and she looks horrified at my appearance. "Millie, your dress. My dear, do you know how much that cost?" She comes up, swiping at me as if she could brush all the dirt off me in seconds.

Who is she even trying to clean me up for? It's just us here. But that's it, isn't it? Even when it's just us, perfection is expected.

I brush her off, slapping her hand away. "Ugh! It's just a dress, Mama! Leave me be! Just leave me!" I turn to catch my father's hate-filled eyes again. "Daddy, I will continue to see Henry—" I glance toward him, but he is already walking down the gravel road. His head is down and back to us. No.

"Henry!" I call, but he doesn't turn around. No. Come back to me. Please.

I struggle to run to him, but my father's grip on my shoulders is too tight. "Stop this foolishness, Millie. He's just a boy. Forget him."

No. He is so much more than just a boy. But they don't see that. They can't see past their idea of what and who they want me to be and be with. They can't see past his tattered clothes and low status. They can't see past their closed minds and social parties.

They don't see what I see.

It doesn't matter. They won't keep me from school. I will love Henry there, and they will never know. It's not like they pay attention to anything I do besides my grades and extracurriculars anyway.

And when we graduate, we'll be free to do what we want. I'll play their game for now, and when Henry and I fly away, we'll make our own rules.

# Chapter Ten

F orget playing by their rules.

I could do it...if I had Henry.

But I don't because he hasn't talked to me since the night of our perfectly horrible date.

Two months ago.

I know what he is thinking. He thinks I'm better off without him. He thinks he isn't good for me and that he can't offer me anything. He thinks if he ignores me that I'll move on and forget him.

But I can't move on.

I have been playing the good little daughter and student like I always have but now that I have experienced what it feels like to be seen, to be my real self, I can't let it go. It's like my first taste of coffee. Before I ever had it, I didn't know what I was missing, but now I've had it and am being denied it... it's all I can think about. It's a drug that I need. I feel like I'm losing my mind.

I quit cheer. I quit student council. I did anything I could to draw attention to myself. I began acting out in my classes, anything to make him look at me. I wanted him to come back to me, to shake me and tell me to stop destroying my life. I wanted him to see that if he thought he was going to destroy my life, I would do it first, and then there wouldn't be anything worse he could do.

I've already done it.

But he hasn't.

He lingers around the school, quiet in the hallways, invisible in the classroom, and worst of all, he won't even look at me.

I just want to scream at him. Look. At. Me! See me. Like you used to. Love me. Like you used to.

How could he forget about me so easily?

I feel myself shattering. The wind beneath my wings is gone and I'm free falling.

"Hey, Millie?" Marryanne comes up next to me in the lunch line. "Are you okay?"

"I'm fine." I grab an apple and put it on my tray. Then scoot down a little, the plastic tray scraping against the metal bars of the lunch line buffet.

"Really? Because you seem... different. Is it that Henry guy who's changed you?"

Her meaning is diminutive, judgmental, but she is right. He has changed me. He has shown me what is real.

"Yeah. It is."

"Well, he doesn't know what he has. You deserve better. Don't let him dumping you get you down. He was trash anyway."

I slam my tray down onto the counter. Drawing attention but I don't care. I feel like a boiling pot of water slowly reaching the top, and no one is looking. All anyone has to do is turn down the heat, but no one truly sees what's in front of them. But now I've just boiled over, and I. Don't. Care.

"Stop. Just stop, Marryanne. You know nothing about him."

She chases me as I storm off and find a seat in the library because I refuse to eat in the lunchroom. I feel overstimulated there now. All the noise and curious eyes. It makes my skin crawl. I hate being looked at... unless it's by him.

"He's from the slums, Millie. His house is literally falling apart. He doesn't even have decent shoes."

I push my tray away, not even hungry anymore. "Oh my God, what is everyone's obsession with his damn shoes. They are just shoes!"

Mrs. Creaton shoots me a glare, promising death if I raise my voice in her library again, and I drop my gaze.

Marryanne throws her hands up. "Jeez, calm down. You're right. They're just shoes... I guess."

"How do you know what his house looks like anyway?"

She sticks a bite of salad into her mouth and speaks with one hand covering her chewing. "I don't, but I've seen him walking home before, and I saw him turn into the Shanty District. All the homes there are falling apart." She shrugs and takes another bite.

"It doesn't matter where he is from. It matters who he is. And he is the best person I know."

"Yeah, well, kindness doesn't pay the bills. If it did, all of us would be poor."

I tune her out as she continues to talk about something to do with the upcoming dance. I couldn't care less about the stupid dance. Who would I go with anyway?

I don't eat any of my lunch or talk to anyone for the rest of the day. I see Henry one time, but when I approach him, he sneaks into the boys' locker room.

Damn him.

He better watch it, though. One of these days, all my ladylike behavior will be thrown out the window, and I will follow him in there. Naked boys be damned. He'll have to talk to me then.

After school, I find that Daddy and Mama are home. Shocker. Truly. They have been gone since last week, and I just didn't care enough to ask when they would be home.

When I walk into the foyer, the first thing I hear is Daddy's voice carrying through the empty halls as he calls me into the dining room. "Millie, come here." His tone saturates the air with disappointment where I used to care. I just don't. I have done nothing but follow all their rules and participate in the activities they deem appropriate for me, yet all I have gotten from them is absence.

So why should I care?

Stepping into the dining room, Daddy is leaning against the fireplace. "You're acting out. I never thought I would see the day my sweet little doll was so defiant." The look in his eyes tells me he cares, but his actions tell me just not enough.

"You've taken notice. That's a first." I roll my eyes and go to leave, but my mother enters, handing Daddy a glass of whiskey.

"Millie. We take notice of everything you do. Mrs. Evelyn told us you quit cheer and the student council. How will that look on your applications?"

"That's exactly my point. *Mrs. Evelyn* told you."

"Is this attitude all from that Polish boy? I knew he was bad for you. You never acted this way before hanging out with him."

I feel the fire crawl up my skin. They don't even realize that I'm trying to tell them how freaking alone I have been all my life, how I have always been exactly what they call me. Their little doll.

They don't see me.

"His name is Henry." I grit out. "And it has nothing to do with him. But since you want to bring him up, he is the only person who knows me. And you have taken him from me. He won't even talk to me now that you have filled his head with lies!" My volume peaks as I scream my frustrations out at them. Frustration at them, at myself. At Henry.

"Lower your voice, Millie. That is not how a lady speaks, especially to their father."

I spin on my heel to face my mother. "Oh, would you just shut up about being a lady! I'm not a lady! I'm not you, and I don't want to be!"

She steps closer to me, keeping her posture perfect and her face a blank mask. "You are a lady, and you will act as such."

"No, Mother, I'm not you. I'm not going to be some quiet little housewife who drinks her martinis and pretends she's happy while being paraded around on the arm of a man who doesn't make her laugh or smile anymore. Do you even love him, Mama? Are you so blinded by your need for designer clothes and expensive pearls that you don't even care that you are wasting your life away with a man who doesn't look at you the way Henry looks at me—"

A sting graces my cheek, and my head snaps to the side.

"Rita," my father says cooly as I bring my hand up to my cheek. Did she just—

"Leave us." He is looking at Mama, but I take the initiative. "Don't bother, Daddy. I'm already gone." Taking the steps two at a time, I run to my room, and surprise, no one follows me. I rip my brown leather suitcase from my chest and begin shoving anything I can reach into it. Extra shoes, socks, jackets. Anything I can think I'll need.

I leave everything I know I'll never need. The pearls, the makeup, the expensive perfumes and Mary Janes. The cashmere scarves and sweater.

I walk out the front door, my parents not even realizing I've left, and make my way down the gravel drive. The trees whisper to me, and I take it as encouragement instead of a warning.

As I get farther and farther into the city, the streets get lighter as the lamps come on, but the eyes on me get darker. Chills race up my spine, and I know I'm not safe, but I'm too stubborn to turn back. I can do this.

Once I find him, I'll be safe.

I turn down the street that leads into the Shanty District, and people stare at me as they pick through trash cans or sit on their porches smoking cigarettes. People young and old gather in groups of three or more, and I understand why as I'm hit with the fact that there is power in numbers, and I'm currently alone.

Shouts ring out from behind closed doors, and bottles crash somewhere in the distance, but I keep walking. I keep looking for him.

About three blocks in, I see him. He's holding a trash bag, and as he closes the lid to the large silver can, I race toward him. "Henry!"

His head turns, his eyes going wide with shock as he rushes up to me, and I jump into his arms.

"Księżniczka, what the hell are you doing here? You can't be here."

"I wanted to see you. I needed to see you. You've been ignoring me, and I'm so mad at you."

"What have you done?" He holds my face in his hands as he looks at me. His eyes travel across my face and down my body, but not in a way that is flirtatious, more like he is making sure I'm not harmed. Shaking his head, he grabs my hand and pulls me toward his house. "Come on, since you're here, let's get you inside. We were just about to eat."

I take in the small room filled with his brothers. They all stare at me as if they are seeing a ghost. The only furniture I see is a small rectangular dining table with mismatched chairs and a two-seater couch. I note that both pieces are located in the kitchen with the table acting as an island of sorts and the couch tucked into the far corner. A curtain is pulled, concealing the corner across from the kitchen, and clothes are hung from the curved rod. There are no televisions, no rugs, no art on the wall, or vases of flowers. It's all so plain but also so... vibrant and warm.

A wood-burning stove sits across from the couch. Oil lamps and candles illuminate the space, and after the initial shock of my arrival, the boys all fall back into easy chatter and laughter.

Tattered shoes are stacked next to the door, and I notice Henry slip off his shoes, and I follow. The contrast of my pristine Mary Janes next to all the dirty brown ones doesn't go unnoticed.

A boy, just older than Henry and me, comes up and leans his body against the wall next to me, looking me up and down with a flirtatious smirk on his face.

"You're really pretty," he says as I take in the dirt on his face and his light brown hair that would probably be blond if washed properly.

"Marcel, git, zostaw ją w spokoju," Henry says as he shoos the boy away.

"Line up," an older boy says. He's about sixteen, I would guess. Like an orchestrated event, all the boys line up in front of the stove, and he begins scooping some kind of soup into mismatched bowls. Each boy takes one, then finds a seat at the table.

Henry pulls me into line, and the boy hands me a bowl, then fills it with soup. I mean to refuse, but honestly, I'm too stunned to really say anything.

I head toward the table, following Henry, and look around, realizing how many chairs surround the small table. It's a tight fit, but I guess they make it work. Nothing like our dining table that has six feet between each chair.

"Here. Henry sits, then guides me to his lap. I go to protest, looking at the empty chair at the head.

"That's for Tato. He'll be home soon," he whispers in my ear, and I blush at his proximity.

"Well, Henry, time to introduce us," one of the older boys says.

Henry nods, then begins. "This is Millie. Millie, this is Michal, Niko, Tomaz, Jakub, and Jan..." He goes around, starting at our left and pointing with his spoon at each of the boys. He skips over the empty chair. "Elijah, Markus, Peter, and Marcel." Marcel sits to our right.

Just as I go to make a polite hello, the front door opens, and Henry's dad walks in. He pauses, a moment of confusion crossing his face, but then he smiles and takes off his jacket. He carries a large brown paper bag, and when he is close enough to the table, he opens it up, dumping out enough golden, puffy, shiny rolls for everyone. Henry hands me one before grabbing another for himself.

His dad then brings over a jar of honey and then sits in the empty chair and looks around the table at his boys. "Dziękuję Bogu za jedzenie, rodzinę... i nowych przyjaciół. Jedzmy."

"Jedzmy," they all repeat, then dig into the soup. I follow, and when the spoon hits my lips, I let out a small moan. "Oh my God. This is amazing."

All the boys' eyes fly to me, and I feel suddenly embarrassed. The older boy across from me, Jan, smiles. "Thank you."

"What's in it? What spices? I've never tasted anything so... flavorful. Is it beef?"

All the boys glance at each other, some smirking while others look confused. "It's just potatoes and black beans in chicken broth," Henry whispers in my ear.

"Oh." My face falls. Right. "Well, it's delicious."

"Księżniczka nie jest przyzwyczajona do tak prostego jedzenia," Jan says and chuckles next to us. Some of the other boys are laughing a little with him. Henry kicks his chair and shoots him a look with his eyes that promises murder.

"Cisza," his father commands cooly. Even though I don't know what he said, I know whatever it was has the boys all looking into their soup and shutting their mouths.

I know whatever Jan said was at my expense, but I can't blame him. I made a silly comment.

"Henry. You start tonight. Since I have a feeling you have much to say."

"Yes, Tato. Uhh...I have no idea what she's doing here. Maybe Millie should start."

He tickles my side and whispers into my ear again. "We always talk about the best and worst part of our day at dinner. You start."

"Oh. Umm." Way to put me on the spot, but I guess I do have some explaining to do. "The best part of my day... well." I think about everything that happened today, cataloging everything into a good and bad pile and realize I have nothing but this moment to put in the good folder.

"I guess right now is the best part of my day. I've never had dinner with a family before. It's... nice. And the worst part... my mother. She..." I reach up to my cheek, still feeling the slight swollenness of the area and the hurt in my heart more than on my face. "We had a misunderstanding."

I meet Alek's eyes and find nothing but warmth in them. "I'm also very sorry for barging in unexpectedly, Mr. Kwiatkowski."

His father's eyes widen, then he smiles and nods. "Excellent pronunciation, Miss Millie. I'm proud of you."

I smile at his praise, feeling more proud of myself than I can ever recall.

"Henry."

"My worst was Mrs. Polina forgetting that she paid me to clean her home while she was away and beating me with her broom when she came home early... Szalona starsza pani." He mumbles the last part and scratches the back of his head. Some laughs filter around the table, and I smile as well, seeing all of the boys looking at Henry. Not just out of obligation but seeming like they are genuinely interested in how his day was.

"The best was..." He looks at me. "Well, introducing you all to Mills."

Each of the boys goes around the table, talking about their day, and we all laugh and curse at some of the bad things they experienced. I can't believe how invested each of them are in each other. It's surreal to see what a family should look like.

They are happier and closer than I have ever been with my own parents, and I envy them.

A knock sounds at the door as we are cleaning up, and Henry's father, who I now know is Aleksander, but he goes by Alek, answers the door.

"Hey, Mr. Kwiatkowski. We have a job for you if you want it. I'm paying double tonight for the late notice."

"I appreciate you thinking of me, but you know my nights are for my boys. If anything comes up during the day tomorrow, you let me know."

"Will do. Just thought I'd ask."

He thanks him and closes the door, going to help Marcel with homework at the table.

"Why didn't he take the job? Don't you all need that money?" I whisper to Henry as I bend down to the bucket of soapy water, which I assume will be to wash clothes.

Henry hands me a bar of soap, and I take it without thinking. "Tato spends all day at work, and nights are reserved for the family. He's big on making sure he spends time with us."

He turned down money... money they desperately need to spend time with his family?

The warm water and soapy suds coat my hand as I help Henry scrub the clothing, but no amount of work I put in changes the appearance of the shirts and pants. Markus and Peter are doing the dishes, and Niko is sweeping the floors.

"Why are you here, Mills?" he asks, his voice laced with worry.

We both speak quietly to keep as much privacy as we can in this small room. But I can tell his brothers, and maybe even his father is listening.

"I missed you. You haven't spoken to me in months, Henry. You told me you loved me, then you left me."

He dips his head, and I can see his jaw tense as he clenches his teeth. "I shouldn't have told you that. I didn't mean it. I'm sorry."

What? That can't be right.

"Nie okłamuj jej," his father says loud enough for us to hear.

"Gówno," Henry whispers. "Trzymaj się z daleka od tego, tato," he says to his father.

I watch his dad dry his hands and then come over and begin washing clothes with us. "He's lying to you. He loves you. And I've watched for two months as he has sulked about the house being a pain in our asses because he's ten times grumpier without you."

"Tato! Zamknij się, proszę!" Henry grits out as a blush creeps up his neck.

I smile at how bold Alek is and how embarrassed Henry is.

"I'll finish up the clothes. Why don't you walk Millie home, syn?"

My eyes fly to Alek's, and I give him my best puppy dog eyes. "Please no. Don't make me go back there."

He gives me a small smile, one that conveys he is definitely going to make me go home. "I'm sorry, Millie. As much as we have enjoyed you with us tonight, you cannot stay. You're a young lady in a house of less-than-appropriate boys. I can't put my boys at risk for what people would say. I'm sorry."

Shoot. I didn't even think of that. My whole body deflates as Henry stands and helps me up off the floor. "Come on, księżniczka. Time to go home."

*I am home*, I want to say but don't. "Fine," I say instead as I follow Henry to the door and put my shoes on.

Henry covers me with his coat as we step into the chilled air. "I don't want to go. I like it at your house."

He laughs. "My house is messy, dirty, more chaotic than anything, and you want to be there more than your own castle on the hill?"

He doesn't take my hand like I'm silently begging him to. He's still keeping his distance. "My castle on the hill is lonely."

Silence hangs in the air. The noises of the Shanty District ring loudly. Two dogs play tug-of-war over a piece of meat that I probably have at least five of stocked in my freezer.

"I-I'm sorry your mom hit you tonight."

I look up at him and see him eyeing the swollen area of my cheek. He brushes his thumb across it. My body breaks out in shivers, and it's not from the cold. "Will you be okay?"

"Yeah. I think it was a fluke. She's never done that before. I think I just revealed a truth to her that she had worked so hard to keep secret, and she lashed out."

"That's no excuse."

"I know."

We walk in silence until we turn out of the Shanty District. I can't go home without knowing things won't continue the way they have been. So it's me who breaks the silence. "Henry, you can't leave me again."

"Mills." He shakes his head and runs his hand down the back of his neck.

"Please, Henry. You're the wind beneath my wings, and I'm flightless without you."

He stops walking, and I turn toward him. I tuck myself into him, making him hold me because I know I'm going to have to push him into this. Finally, he wraps his arms around me and places a kiss on my forehead.

"Come back to me," I whisper into his chest, breathing in the scent that is my Henry.

I feel it when his body relaxes, melting into my own. He releases a breath he was holding tight in his chest.

He relents.

"I could never truly leave you, księżniczka."

## Chapter Eleven

"**Y**ou told me you wouldn't leave me again." Tears stream down my face as I cling to Henry. His small bag is packed and carelessly slung over his shoulder. I bawled my eyes out when he told me he was joining the Marine Corps after graduation, and I don't think I've stopped since.

"Syn, take care of yourself." His father stands in front of us, his hands tucked into the pocket of his jeans. He is calm and under control, as he always is, and I'm a mess. Never under control. Like I always am.

"I will, Tato." Henry glances around the bus station, seeing that it's only his dad and me to see him off. His brothers didn't agree with his decision to join the military. They see it as him abandoning them and not staying home to take care of the family. Honestly, I think they're afraid, just like I am. Scared that he will be another casket coming home with a flag over the top.

"Give them time. They will come around," Alek reassures with little confidence in his eyes.

"If you say so."

Henry and I have been together for four years. When other cou-
ples split up, got back together, and split up again, we remained
steady.

I have spent more time with Henry's family than my own. My
parents and I still don't see eye to eye. They are furious that I decided
not to attend an Ivy League... now that women can actually attend.

As soon as we both turned eighteen, we married. Of course my
parents refused to attend. It was only Tato and Henry's brothers.
Not even my so-called friends showed, but in the end, it didn't
matter. All I needed was him. We have been husband and wife for
one month, and now he is leaving me. But as soon as he graduates
from boot camp, I'll be there, and we'll start our lives. We will find
a little house or apartment wherever he is stationed. I'll attend a
local community college and get a degree in business. We'll start our
family. We'll be free.

As we finished high school over the years, Henry has become
even more antisocial. In fact, we both have. We realized all we really needed was one another. Although I at least remained friendly,
Henry practically pummels anyone who looks at me wrong. I think
all those years ago when I was attacked lives in his mind still today.
He's terrified of me being hurt but even more scared of not being
able to protect me. I thought he would have let it go, but he carries
it with him still.

I also think that exact thought is a large part of why he wanted to
join the Marines. He wants to feel prepared to care for me not only
physically but also financially.

I tried to convince him to go to college with me. We could open our little coffee shop, work, and live simply until we could afford more, but he said the military would be the only secure and reliable source of money. He isn't wrong, but I would live on the streets before I would live without him. If he dies over there because he was trying to give me the best life possible... I don't know what I would do. But no manner of convincing is budging the stubborn, stubborn boy.

"I can see you worrying, księżniczka. It's just boot camp."

"Well, what happens after boot camp, huh? You go off to fight that silly war."

"I'll always come back to you." He wraps me in a hug, and I take in a large breath of this scent. Still that oil and firewood that always lingers on his clothes from home.

"I'll write to you as soon as I can."

"I'll be waiting."

He turns to embrace his father in a hug and climbs the steps to the large Greyhound bus that will take him away from me.

I try to rein in my tears, but they just fall and fall and fall.

"It's going to be okay. He's tough," Alek says, I think more to himself than to me as he wraps me in a hug.

"But I'm not."

Henry and I have had a whirlwind of a love story. I knew the first moment I launched that rock at him that I would never be able to get him out of my head and my heart. And like two speeding trains, we collided, and my heart has not been mine since. Many have said we wouldn't last. My friends and parents tried to convince me to end "my silly little fantasy" a multitude of times, but they don't know what we have. How could they? You don't know the feeling of truly finding your soulmate until they walk into your life. Then, to everyone else, it happens too fast, but to you, it feels like you've known them forever. Because you have; they are part of your soul.

I don't even remember what life was like without him.

He sees me when no one else ever does. He held me to no expectations except to just be myself. He challenged me, accepted me, tormented me, and eradicated any insecurity or fears that I had.

We have spent the past four years at the fair every summer, going to the ballet or movies. Although those dates were only once a year, on my birthday, they meant the world to me. Mostly we just spent time together, among his brothers or at the little coffee shop we frequented. In fact, we were there so much that Marla, the owner, offered Henry and me jobs. That's where we have both been working for the past two years.

I have soaked in knowledge about the business like a sponge. I love creating new drinks and flavors, and although Marla refuses to add them to the menu, saying they are "too out there," whatever that means... Henry and I enjoy my creations.

My favorite flavor is hazelnut. Henry says his is the same, but I think he only likes it because I do. I'm going to miss our morning coffee.

"Well, Millie. Would you like to go eat some lunch? I think Jakub is making pierogi."

"With all due respect, Tato, if I see any of your sons right now, I'm going to punch them in their faces. How could they not see Henry off?" I feel my anger rising, and I'm almost positive steam is coming from my ears.

I stop as the bus passes on our walk, and I wave to Henry, who has his hand pressed to the glass. Alek begins walking again as I stand frozen, trying to take a photograph of that moment and store it in my brain.

He just chuckles as he turns back toward the street that leads to the Shanty District. "Come by for dinner, then? When you're less hostile."

"I'm always hostile, Tato." I chase him, then loop my arm through his. "But Jakub's pierogi is my favorite, so he is the only one I forgive right now."

*September 22, 1968*

*Księżniczka,*

*It's been one week of hell.*

*Boot camp is nothing as I expected it would be. As soon as we got off the bus, the sergeants were in our faces, calling us maggots and treating us no better. I'm pretty sure I constantly have spit covering my face.*

*The physical work is excruciating. I always thought I was pretty fit, but boy, was I wrong. In one week, three guys have already been sent to the medical rehab platoon with broken legs or arms.*

*It's been one week, and I don't think you would recognize me. All our heads were shaved almost immediately. We all look the same. We are not human while we are recruits.*

*I also have a new name. I haven't been Henry since I got on that bus. Now I'm Ski. My Polish surname is too long and difficult to pronounce, so it's been shortened. But I'm actually okay with it. It has a nice ring to it, doesn't it?*

*I miss you like crazy. The coffee here is shit. Oh that's also a bad habit I have already picked up. Every other word out of these guys' mouths are curse words, and I have begun to speak similarly.*

*I miss our coffee dates, and the first thing I want when I graduate is a hazelnut coffee with you. My letters may not come as frequently as I had hoped. We barely get time here to write. I'm going to dedicate my Sundays to writing to you and resting. And I'm not sure how long it will take my letters to get to you, but I'll keep writing them.*

*Now, I have to come clean about something. When I left, you asked me what I would be doing in the Marines, and I told you I wasn't sure. But that was a lie. Really, I was scared to tell you. I didn't want you to worry about it, but now I have to tell you.*

*I'm going to be a machine gunner. It's really the only MOS that I felt I would be good at. You know I'm a good shot, and it's the place I feel I can serve the best. Because of that, I will have some additional training to go through. After my nine weeks here, I'll head off to infantry training for four weeks, then another four with my MOS.*

*Please don't hate me when I get back to you. I'm sorry I had to lie.*

*I love you, Mills.*

*You're the wind beneath my wings.*

*-Always*

*Your Henry*

# january 12<sup>th</sup>, 1969

"O of." Henry lets out as he catches me. His laughter fills my chest and soothes every crack in my heart I had obtained in the last seventeen weeks. As soon as I was able, I bolted to him, running and jumping into his arms. I told myself I would act like an appropriate lady, the prim and proper wife, but forget that. I wasn't prim or proper, I sure as hell wasn't a lady, and I missed him.

"Oww, ow! Is that Ski's wife!? Damn, Ski. Look at you go, man!" His buddies whistle and laugh, but I don't care. Nothing matters except him holding me. Finally.

He moved from Parris Island to Camp Pendleton, and when I heard, I hopped on a bus right away and found a long-term hotel until we could move into family housing.

When he releases me, my feet hitting the black pavement of Camp Pendleton, I take in his white hat with the gold Marine Corp emblem, the black jacket with white belt and deep blue pants. The Marine Corps uniform is a sight for sore eyes on Henry.

Now that I'm finally taking in all of him, he looks drastically different, but his eyes are the same. His hair is buzzed short, his face slimmer, and body more toned than before.

"I missed you, księżniczka," he says as he bumps his nose to mine.

"I know." I wrap my arms around him again, feeling like I can't get close enough.

His body shakes with his laughter. "Aren't you going to kiss me?"

I pull him in with force, and our lips meet. After so long, I thought he would taste different, but he doesn't.

"You taste like hazelnuts," he practically purrs. "God, it's been too long since I have had decent coffee."

"Then let's get you your fix, shall we?"

"Take me away," he says with that smile of his that I missed so damn much.

I loop my arm through his right arm, and he removes it. I glare at him... how dare he not want—but then he moves me and threads my arm through his left arm. "I need to keep my right arm free to salute."

"Oh, that's—okay." I tuck my chin. What a strange rule. Maybe I should act a bit more proper.

We stopped into a coffee shop I have been frequenting while I waited for boot camp to finish and order my usual. Henry practically cries at the taste of the coffee, and it makes me giggle.

I see the women around us eyeing him, and my jealousy rages inside my chest. I never had to worry about other women looking at him. He was never the type to draw attention, and now that he has it, I don't like it.

But they can look all they want. He is mine, and that gold band on his finger lets the world know it.

"Simmer, księżniczka. You look like you are about to jump over the counter and strangle our server."

"If she doesn't keep her eyes to herself, I just might." I narrow my eyes at her, but she doesn't see because all she can look at is my husband.

Henry grips my chin with his thumb and forefinger and pulls my face to look at him, then gives me a kiss on my nose. "And she can look all she wants. I'm yours."

We stare into each other's eyes for what feels like forever before he looks down at his lap. I can see the change in his expression, the air around him, his body language. There is something he isn't telling me.

"Mills. I..." He pauses. Longer than I'm comfortable with. My heart pounds, as if trying to escape my own chest and climb into his. God, what is it?

"I..." He swallows hard and takes a deep breath. "They are sending me to Nam sooner than I had expected."

No.

I just got him back.

"How soon," I say as the tears build behind my eyes. We haven't even been able to start our lives together yet.

"Next week," he whispers as he looks up, meeting my eyes.

"For how long?"

"Thirteen months."

My world crashes down. I stop breathing momentarily, then tip my chin and hold my head high. I knew this was coming. I knew as a Marine's wife, he would belong to them first. I try to bite my lip to keep the tears from falling, but I'm not able to, and one drips down my cheek. Before it hits my chin, Henry kisses it away, gently brushing the corner of my mouth.

"Then we will enjoy the week we have." I try to fill my voice with as much strength as I can, but I'm shattering on the inside. One week. That's all we have for the next thirteen months, maybe ever.

"Oh. I plan on enjoying you very much, księżniczka."

A blush creeps up my cheeks. After all the years of being with him, he still makes butterflies erupt in my stomach. He still makes me soar higher than any bird could fly. And I don't know what I will do without him for so long, but I can survive any amount of time if it means he comes back to me.

He has to come back to me. He has to.

"Will you do something for me?" His hand grabs mine as he brings it to his lips, leaving kisses against each pad of my fingers.

"Anything."

"Will you dance with me? Tonight? There is a celebratory ball. I'd love if you would go with me."

A ball? Henry and I have never been to a dance or a ball. They had them in high school, but I never asked Henry to go, and he never asked me. We both knew that we would rather save our money than spend it on dresses or suits. We would dance to the radio in his father's kitchen, dance at the fair, or even just dance to the music in our heads late at night when no one was around. But a formal ball? Never.

"I'll go anywhere with you," I say as his eyes light up. Mischief and danger flit inside those irises, and I know I'm in for one hell of a night.

Later that night, I'm in a light blue floor-length dress, and he is in his dress blues as he spins me around a grand ballroom in one of the hotels here in San Diego. Marines fill the space, and I can't help but wonder, among all the smiling and laughing, how many of these Marines won't make it home. For how many will this be their last dance?

I send a prayer to a God I haven't spoken to in a while that it won't be Henry's last.

And here I go again, crying like a big baby.

I'm a Marine's wife. I need to be stronger.

"Księżniczka, why are you crying?" He leans his forehead against mine as the song turns slow, and the band plays Elvis Presley's "Can't Help Falling in Love with You."

"Come back to me, Henry," I beg. My voice breaks as I say the prayer out loud.

"I'll never truly leave you, Mills. I want you to promise me, promise me you'll find me every day and you'll hold those moments close. Find me in the sunrise when it streams through the window and hits your cheek. Imagine it's my kiss. Find me in the hazelnut coffee as you sip it each morning, remembering the taste of my lips. Find me in the touch of the breeze as it brushes your hair across your back and feel my touch. I'll never truly leave you."

"Promise me, Henry. Promise me that you were meant to fly, and you will not die."

His warm hands hold me tighter, pulling my body into his. "Baby, I can't make that promise. But if I'm meant to die, it was one hell of a good flight."

*September 11, 1969*

*My księżniczka,*

*Do you remember the first letter I wrote you in boot camp? I told you I was in hell.*

*I was wrong.*

*Now, I'm in hell.*

*We are up before the sun, cleaning and oiling our guns, and don't sleep till late in the night if at all. The fear, Mills, the fear is like nothing I've ever felt. You know where I come from, but fear of cold, of hunger cannot compare to the fear of being in the bush. And it's constant. It never ends.*

*The gunfire rings in my ears and haunts the few dreams I have. But there is no solace in the silence either. The silence is still and heavy. Every branch breaking or whisper of the bush in the wind reminds us that they are out there.*

*And the faces, Mills. They haunt me. The faces of the children. The women. Even the men that my bullet has found haunt me. I know this is war. I know it's me or them. I know that, but it doesn't change the fact that I have killed. I have killed so many. Sometimes I don't even know where my bullet lands. Sometimes I don't even know who I am anymore.*

*I've held my brothers as they've died. I've thanked God it wasn't me. And I've begged God to let it be me instead.*

*But the worst is being away from you.*

*God, Mills, I crave your touch. Your smell is lost to me. I never thought I would forget the sound of your voice, but I am. It's drifting every day, and I'm fighting to hold on to you. When I first got here, the men who had been here months already told me I would forget. Forget the taste of my woman, the feel of her, the sound of her. They told me I would forget, and I swore they were wrong.*

*But they weren't.*

*It's not you I'm forgetting, but all that makes you mine.*

*Any day now, all I'll have left of you is the photo I keep in my helmet.*

*Don't let me go, Mills.*

*Come back to me.*

*-Always*

*Ski*

# april 1971

*K*nock. *Knock. Knock.*

The sound echoes through the small house, waking me just before my alarm. Who the hell could be here this early? I don't think I was expecting anyone, but between my college classes and working full-time at the coffee shop, I might have forgotten.

Swinging my robe around my shoulder, I shiver as the warm cotton envelopes me. I tie it securely at my waist and rub the sleep from my eyes as I approach the door.

Just before opening the solid wood, a heaviness hits my chest, making me pause, but I push it away. Chalking it up to stress, I shake my head and take a deep breath, which usually helps. I've been getting that feeling in my chest often the last week or so, but I figure it's not uncommon with the mental and emotional load I currently have on my plate.

I turn the handle and swing the door wide.

Two Marines in Dress Blues stand at my door.

No.

"No. No. No. No. Please... please don't—"

"Mrs. Kwiatkowski?"

"Don't."

"I'm sorry to inform you that Lance Corporal Henry Stephen Kwiatkowski has been classified as missing in action."

*Missing.*

It filters in slowly through the wall I had immediately erected at the sight of the two Marines.

"He's not dead?"

"We cannot confirm at this time. His helicopter went down behind enemy lines."

"Behind enemy lines?"

I straighten my robe and smooth out my curls. Okay, I can do this. This is what I have accepted and been prepared for. At least he isn't dead.

"Thank you. When will I know more?"

"You will be notified as soon as we know anything. I advise staying close to the phone."

"Okay. Okay. Yes. I can do that. Thank you."

They nod their heads at me and turn to leave. I softly close the door, and when it's fully sealed. I break. Sinking to the floor, I bury my head in my hands and sob until the tears stop coming. The entire time, Henry's words from so long ago play through my mind on a constant loop. *If she's meant to fly, she will. If she's meant to die, she will.*

But he didn't die. Yet. He's meant to fly.

One agonizingly long week later, the phone rings, and I jump at the receiver. "Hello?"

"God, your voice, księżniczka." His voice is scratchy like he just woke up or hasn't used his voice in a while.

"Henry! Oh my God! Are you okay?"

He chuckles, and I laugh with relief. God, to hear his voice, his laugh. "It hurts like hell. But I'm better now."

"What happened?"

"I-I don't want to talk about that right now, baby. I only have a few minutes."

"Okay. When will you be home?" My body practically falls into the small wooden chair next to our table that I have yet to eat with Henry at.

"Mills."

I know that tone. That's the tone he uses when he knows he's either about to piss me off or ruin my day.

"I-I'm going back."

What? He can't go back!

"What the hell are you talking about, Henry Stephen?"

"My injuries are healed. I-I'm able to go back, and I am. I can't leave my brothers. My platoon is still out there. So I should be too."

"No, you should be home. With me. Please, Henry," I plead with him.

"I'm sorry, Mills. But I belong out there right now. I can't leave my brothers behind."

Then it hits me. He isn't talking like he didn't have a choice. He is speaking as if he made this decision himself.

"Did you choose this? Henry, tell me right now you didn't have a choice. Tell me that you weren't given the opportunity to come home, and you chose to return to that war."

Silence rings loud over the receiver.

"Tell me." My back teeth stay closed because if I let them loose, I'll break fully.

"I can't tell you that, Mills. I have to go. I love you, and I'll see you soon."

"Wait!" I'm so angry with him right now, but I don't know when I'll get to speak to him again. If I will get to speak to him again. "Come back to me."

"I'll never truly leave you."

The phone line goes dead, and the thoughts in my mind race. How could he choose to go back there? How could he want to be there instead of at home with me? How? Why?

One of the Marine wives I met when I first moved into family housing told me something that I thought I would never understand, but now I do more than ever. The conversation plays through my mind like a movie.

*"I haven't seen you here before. Is this your first duty station?" A red-headed woman, a little older than me, says as we wait in line at the commissary.*

*"Yes. You?"*

*"Oh no. My husband's been in the Marines for eight years now. This is our fourth."*

*"Wow. Eight years? How do you do it? Any advice for a new military wife?"*

*She dips her head, and when she looks back up at me, her friendly smile is gone. Instead, there is sorrow in her eyes but also a strength. She is not a quiet little housewife. She is a Marine's wife.*

*"You'll never truly have him again. Once he goes to war, he will belong to his brothers. He will choose his brothers. And even if his body comes home, living and breathing, a part of him will always stay there."*

*I look down at the bananas and the bag of rice, the Polish sausage, and the carton of milk in my basket. I refuse to believe that, though. Henry has always been mine. He is strong. He may be different when he comes home, but he will still be by my Henry.*

*"I can see the hope in your smile, my dear girl. That hope will get you through his deployments. But when he comes home, remember that no matter who he comes home as, he will need you. He will need you to save him from his mind, to remind him that it shouldn't have been him. To survive his absence, you detach, and when he does come home, you latch onto him. That is the job of a Marine's wife. He fights with a gun; we fight with our hearts."*

I will never be able to understand his mind. But I know his heart. I have to trust that he has made this decision because he knows it's what is right. The selfish side of me isn't ready to share him, but that's what I've been doing ever since that day he stepped onto that Greyhound, isn't it?

I pick myself up off the floor, telling myself I'll never see him again. If I live in a world where he is already gone, will it make it easier when he doesn't come back? If I tell myself that every time I read his letter, it will be the last one, will I be able to survive the torment of never knowing if he is lying on Vietnam soil, bleeding out?

I will detach to survive, just like she said. And when he comes home, it will be my time to fight.

# september 1972

*Whoosh, whoosh, whoosh, whoosh.*

The repetitive sound of the fan blades rotating above our bed pulls me fully from sleep. But something is off. Even in my sleep, my body knows something isn't right. I lift my head from my pillow, looking over at Henry's side of the bed, but he isn't there.

He has been home from Vietnam for a little over a year, and this month he got out of the Marine Corps. He didn't sign on for another reenlistment.

But just like the woman from the commissary said, he isn't home. Yes, his body sleeps next to me at night, we drink coffee in the mornings and evenings, go grocery shopping together, and go to the cinema. He dances with me in the kitchen, laughing and smiling, but then just as quickly, the smile falls, and his eyes are lost.

His heart is home with me, but his mind is still in Vietnam.

He's different. He wakes before the sun. He doesn't sleep at night. He makes six or seven patrols around the house before he comes in and locks all the doors, then double-checks the locks ten minutes later. He can't stand for the house to be silent, so he always has the

TV or radio playing, and at night, it's worse. When the house falls quiet, he can't sit still.

He doesn't like to leave the house, but he does for me. He is torn between protecting his peace by isolating himself and protecting me. And when we venture into town, we drive past the protestors. They spit on him when we walk the streets, just trying to enjoy our day. They call him a traitor, and I see his fist clench at his sides, but he holds his tongue.

"Henry?" I walk out into the living room as I tie my robe at the waist. Then the kitchen, the bathroom, and even the garage. But he isn't in the house. The doors are all locked, so where is he?

As I'm walking past the dining room, I see through our windows a man standing in the front yard. I jump, clutching my hand to my chest. "Oh my—"

But then I notice the shotgun in his hands. He isn't facing the house. But away from it like he's...protecting it.

"Oh, Henry," I whisper as the click of the lock echoes through the house. The night air sweeps in, and my body breaks out in shivers. Clutching my robe tighter, I slowly approach him.

A twig snaps below my foot as I step into the cold grass, and the snap resounds around us.

Henry spins faster than I have ever seen him move, and suddenly, I'm looking down the barrel of a gun pointed at me by my husband. By the boy I fell in love with at fourteen.

"Henry." My voice breaks as tears fill my eyes. My heart pounds in my chest.

He lowers the gun and steps into me, pulling me behind him as he turns to face the trees again. Our small house faces a small park. The trees that line the park are thick and look like a small forest.

"Mills, what are you doing here? You must go back inside." His voice is urgent as if he is scared for me.

"Henry, come inside."

"I can't." He is clutching the gun to his chest. "The trees are whispering to me, Mills. Warning me. They're out there. Waiting in the bush. I won't let them have you."

"Henry. There is no one out there." I lay my hand on his bicep, and he flinches away.

"You don't know, Millie!" he whispers, trying to keep his voice quiet. "That's what they want you to think. They will wait for hours. For days, they will wait. That's what they're doing. Waiting for us to sleep."

I round to his front, and he tries to push me behind him again. But I don't let him. Grabbing his sweet face in my palms, I pull his forehead to mine. "Come back to me," I whisper to him as the barrel of the gun presses against our chests, and tears slip down my cheeks.

"Come back to me," I say it over and over. A prayer repeated with as much faith as I can hold on to anymore.

"Come back to me. Come back to me."

When he pulls back, his blue eyes meet mine, and I can see he's my Henry again. Tears stream down his face as he looks at me with nothing but terror shining through those glacial eyes, then down at the gun gripped into his hand. "Oh God. I'm so sorry, księżniczka. Did I—Are you—" He stutters as his eyes roam my body.

"I'm okay. You didn't hurt me." I grab his arm and begin pulling him inside.

"I heard the blades. The blades of the helo, they woke me up, and I—"

"I know. But you came back to me."

He stays silent, his brows furrowed as if he is confused. He slips in and out of these moments more often than he realizes. But this is the first time I have seen him recognize just how lost he truly is.

Before we step back into the house, he looks over his shoulder one more time. His eyes scan the trees.

I walk him to the dining table and put on a pot of coffee. I know he won't sleep. He lights a cigarette and pulls out his deck of cards from his shirt pocket. Shuffling them over and over again. The repetitive motion is something he does often. I think it's a way to calm himself.

I watch the muscles of his arms flex under the Devil Dog tattoo he has on his arm between his elbow and wrist. Something he got overseas with his brothers.

"Will you talk to me?"

He looks up from staring into his coffee as I sit across from him at our little table. The early morning is still dark outside, and the small lamp on the kitchen counter illuminates the right side of his face. The smell of his cigarette and hazelnut coffee fills the space.

"I can't, Mills."

"Why not? How am I supposed to help you through this when I can't understand."

"It doesn't matter. Even if I could tell you, you would never understand. But I can't even say the words—the memories. They..."

He stops. I bow my head. I'm trying to be understanding. I'm trying to help, but I don't know how. I'm fighting to keep his heart intact when his mind is fractured, but I don't know how.

Standing from my chair, I step between his legs and take his hands, wrapping them around my waist as he settles his heavy head against my stomach. We hold each other. Recentering ourselves.

"I am here, Henry. I will always be here. Every time you drift, I will call you back to me. You were meant to fly, and I will be the wind beneath your wings."

"You are the wind beneath my wings," he chants.

"We will get through this just as we have everything else in our lives. Together." I brush my hands over his buzzed head, feeling the soft short strands and think about all the times I've done this same movement except before it was through longer, deep brown strands. But no matter what changes this man goes through, it will only ever be my hands who hold him.

I will grow with him.

Grieve with him.

Hope with him.

And I will die by his side.

# 1994

"Mills! Customer!" Henry calls from the front. I was in the back restocking, but he always prefers for me to handle the customers. He prefers to stick to himself and make the coffee. Which I'm okay with. I love getting to know our loyal coffee addicts.

We opened up Mill's Coffee House about five years ago, shortly after we moved to this quiet little Oregon town. We needed to get out of the city. Henry wasn't doing well with the commotion and noise. He needed peace, so we moved around a few places, and as we were traveling the Oregon coast one year, we came upon this little town. Aurora, Oregon, was everything I had dreamed of.

It's small, quiet, and friendly. Not too far from a big city so we can still attend the ballet and concerts but far enough where you feel the peace along the dirt roads. I thought it would be the perfect place to start a family, but... well, that never happened for us. I struggled for years with not being able to get pregnant until I finally went to the doctor and found out that was never going to happen for us.

"Coming!" I make my way to the front counter. "We really need to get a damn bell. I can never hear when someone comes in," I mumble to Henry as he is pouring more beans into the grinder.

"I'll make it happen," he says right before placing a kiss to my cheek.

"Hi, how can I help you today, dear?" The small thing can't be more than eighteen or nineteen, and I've never seen her come by before. She must be new in town or passing through.

One of my favorite things about being the only coffee shop in town is the variety of people we see. I love to know their stories, and I make it a point to converse with our customers. We are a family here at Mill's.

She brushes her long black hair out of her face. She is beautiful. Green eyes, high cheekbones, dainty little nose.

"An Americano, please." She hands me the cash, and I can already hear Henry behind me firing up the espresso machine.

"And a name for the order, love."

"Evangeline."

"Evangeline. Like an angel," I say as I write her name on the cup. Even though she is the only customer currently, writing the name helps me remember.

"Huh?" she says confused.

"Like an angel. Your name. It means like an angel. It's one of my favorite names." I smile at her and hand the cup to Henry.

"Oh. I-I didn't know that. Thank you." Her voice is timid and quiet.

"Where are you from, Evangeline?" I move down the counter, and she follows. I motion to one of the barstools that sits just next to the register so I can continue our conversation as she waits for her drink.

"I just moved here with my husband. I'm from Portland, though."

"Is your husband from here?" I take a blueberry muffin from the case and set it on a plate, then slide it in front of her.

"Oh." She goes to protest, but I wave at her dismissively. "On the house."

"Thank you." She bites into it and moans as the delicious taste hits her tongue.

"My secret recipe." I wink at her, and she smiles with her mouth full. Her hand comes up to cover her mouth, and she says, "You probably know him. Vincent Eros."

"Oh. Yes, you are Dr. Eros's wife? He told me about meeting someone in Portland."

I would never say it to her, but I was fearful for the woman Vincent set his sights on. He is a kind man to the public, but I know broken eyes when I see them. Whatever that man has been through, he hides it, and that is the worst thing one can do. He walks around this little town, practically owning it since he is one of the only doctors, and his best friend is the mayor. He pretends he's normal, but something is off with him.

"If you don't mind me asking, sweetie. How old are you?"

Dr. Eros is... around twenty-seven or twenty-eight. And she doesn't even look old enough to drink.

"I'm eighteen. Almost nineteen." She pauses, swallowing the bite she was chewing. Her eyes find the wrapper as she nervously plays with it. "I know what you're thinking. Everyone does. Married to a man nine years older than me. But he—he loves me, and I love him. He really helped me out of a difficult situation when I was seventeen, and the relationship just grew."

"I see. Well, welcome to town."

Henry hands her the Americano and nods his head. I stick my elbow into his side and encourage him with my eyes to introduce himself.

Something about this girl tells me that she is going to need us.

"Ski." He wipes his hand on the towel that is thrown over his shoulder, then sticks it out to her. Her small hand dwarfs his own aged hand.

"Evangeline Eros."

"That's a long name. Mind if I call you Angel?"

"Angel..." She says it like she is considering it. Trying it on for taste. "I like it."

"What are your plans now that you're here?" I ask, hoping she doesn't say stay-at-home wife...

"I'm starting college, actually. I'm getting my teaching credentials, and I hope to teach elementary school."

She sips her coffee and comments about how delicious it is, but you don't have to tell us that. We are well aware of how good our coffee is. Henry excuses himself and goes to the back after wishing her a good day.

"Well, you stop in here each morning before classes, and I'll make sure you get the best coffee on the house. But you have to promise you'll stop by. Every morning, I want to see that beautiful face."

"Of course," she says as she gets up and leaves.

There is a pressure in my chest that pulls at me to listen. There is something about her that draws at my motherly instincts. She needs to be protected.

"You cannot adopt her," Henry says, and I turn to see him leaning against the doorframe, arms crossed. He never lost his muscular physique when he got out of the Marines. He began running each morning and evening, and I think that not only helped keep his body in shape but his mind as well.

Over the years, his mind has drifted less and less. He has begun to open up to me, telling me stories of his time in Vietnam. His brothers who didn't make it home. It crushed me when he admitted that he often thinks it should have been him. But I stay steady in reminding him if they are meant to fly, they will. And he always finishes with if they are meant to die, they will.

He was not meant to die.

And there is a reason for that.

God is not done with him. He has a purpose here on Earth, even if he doesn't know it himself yet.

"Pfft." I wave my hand at him. "I don't know what you mean."

"You have that look in your eyes."

"She is married to Vincent Eros. I just want to keep an eye on her. There's no harm in that."

"No meddling, księżniczka." He comes up and wraps his arm around my shoulders and pulls me in for a kiss. "If she's meant to fly…"

"She will," I finish for him.

"Close up, księżniczka. We need to leave for your appointment soon." Henry gives me one more kiss to the forehead, then turns to the front door and flips the sign to Closed.

I have a doctor's appointment in Portland for a small dimple I noticed in my breast a few weeks ago. I brushed it off as nothing, telling Henry that breasts change as we get older, but he has been insistent that I get it checked out. He's such a worrier. So to get him off my case, I scheduled an appointment, and he hasn't let me forget.

"Fine. But you owe me ice cream when we're done."

"Are you five?"

"No ice cream. No doctor."

"Fine. Jesteś dla mnie takim wrzodem na dupie," he says as he shuts down the machines and begins cleaning them. Taking the towel from my waist, I whip it at him, and it hits him in the hip.

"Oh, you've done it now, księżniczka." Those blue eyes turn hungry as he stalks toward me, and I take off around the counter, but the chase doesn't last long as he wraps his arms around my waist.

The cold counter hits the backs of my legs, seeping through my dress, and he stands between my open knees. We kiss like it's the last time, savoring every moment.

Then off to the doctor we go.

# 1995

E vangeline is sitting across from me in the shop. Her hands shake as I break the news to her. "It's an aggressive form, Angel. I'm afraid treatment has not been as successful as we had hoped and... well, frankly, I'm tired."

"Millie." The tears rim her eyes. My sweet Evangeline has been here consistently since the first day she walked through our doors. She has become like the daughter we were never blessed with.

"Don't cry for me, sweetie. Henry and I have this saying, something we have told each other since we were kids. If we are meant to fly, we will. If we are meant to die, we will. I had a beautiful flight, and I'm ready. I've accepted it, dear. But I'm fearful for Henry. He won't let me go when it's time, and I need you to be there for him."

Henry has been relentless in his search for a cure. For treatment that will help. He has been calling doctors all around the United States, but all have told him the same thing. Nothing more can be done. I just want to live the rest of my days in peace with him. Dancing in our kitchen, drinking our morning coffee, and snuggling up on the couch to watch our favorite movies.

My biggest fear is that he will join me too soon when I die. He will chase me to the other side, and I cannot allow that. He must fly. He was meant to.

"My Angel..." I take her hand in mine. "Do not let him retreat into his mind. Do not let the demons have him. You have to be here. Everyday. I need you to look after him."

"Millie. I don't know what little ole me can do for him. You are his soulmate."

"And you are his daughter. Maybe not in blood but in his heart. He will continue for you. Promise me."

"I promise."

Evangeline has been a constant in our lives, and even though Henry pretends she doesn't mean the world to him, she does. I see it in the way he watches Vincent when he's around the shop. The way he asks her frequently how things are at home. How he sits and helps her with her coursework and the way he laughs with her as she continues to butcher the pronunciation of the Polish phrases he teaches her.

When I'm gone, Henry will be alone. His father passed away years ago and he never mended the relationships with his brothers. They've sent a few letters over the years, but they haven't spoken in person since the day Henry joined the Marines.

He needs Evangeline. And she needs him.

"I hate to interrupt your girl time, but can I borrow my wife?" Henry's deep voice interrupts us, and I smile at his presence, the serenity that always washes over me when he is near.

"Of course." Evangeline stands and embraces me in a hug. I adjust the beanie that I wear to keep my head warm. Now that I no longer have any hair from the treatments, I find that I'm cold all the time.

"I just got off the phone with another doctor from New York. He said that he could see us in a month. He told me the same thing about your form of breast cancer but said he would be willing to do an assessment and review your file more close—"

"Henry." My hand to his cheek halts him. "I'm tired. I don't want to travel to New York. I just want to be here, with you."

His jaw tenses, the muscles rippling, even under the beard he has been growing the last few years. "But the doctors here aren't able to—""Henry. I'm not going. Listen to me. I'm tired. I know what you are doing, and I can't anymore."

"Księżniczka." The tears fall from his crystal-blue eyes. Eyes that are more tired than I have ever seen them. "I can't do this without you," he confesses as his nose bumps mine.

"Yes, you can. Henry, you made me fly so high. Now you must let me—"

"Stop. Don't you dare say it."

He grasps my face in his warm hands, and I notice how they seem much larger than before. His forehead comes to mine, and our lips brush. I feel the wetness of his tears drip down his cheeks, following the curves of his face to settle on the corner of his lips, and I kiss them away.

"Will you dance with me?" I whisper against his lips.

"Right now?"

"Yes."

He doesn't respond with his words but pulls me in close, his arms wrapping around my waist. My arms around his neck can barely reach, and I just don't have the energy to stand on my tiptoes like I used to when we would dance this way.

As he always has, noticing the smallest details, he picks me up so I can wrap my legs around him and save my energy. We sway and move, right in the center of our coffee shop, and he begins singing softly in my ear. The song we danced to the night he graduated boot camp transports me back to a time we were both young and healthy, we had our whole lives ahead of us. Now, I'm on borrowed time but Henry holding me makes everything magical and beautiful once again.

# evangeline | 1998

"Angel, we must return home. Ski can meet Gage later." My husband grips the steering wheel, his knuckles turning white. I know he is frustrated; he hates when I spend time with Ski. But after Millie died, I couldn't leave him. Actually, I began going more often. In the morning before school and in the evenings after.

I have one year left before I graduate with my bachelor's in education, and then I already have a job lined up at the local elementary school. And once my course load isn't as heavy, I plan to work part-time at the shop so I can spend even more time with Ski. He even set up a crib and play area in the back office for Gage.

He has become the father figure I never had. The grandpa that my child will have.

"Yes, he must meet my son. I promised I would bring him by as soon as I could."

"Our son, Evangeline," Vincent scolds.

"Oh, you know what I meant." I wave him off, but I see the darkness in his eyes.

Vincent has always had a side to him that he keeps buried, and I've always been okay with that. It was just me after all, and he has never done anything to hurt me. He doesn't physically abuse me; he doesn't even raise his voice at me. I'm his world. At least that's what he always says.

I notice it, though. The darkness.

To say I haven't thought about the implications of bringing children into our life with him being... different would be a lie, but God had other plans, and one day, my period was late.

But I don't regret it. The first time I felt my son move inside my belly, I fell in love. And even if his father had demons, Gage would have me. For infinity, I will be there for him. I will protect him.

"Come on, please Vin, for me?" I pout my bottom lip, and I see him melt. He always does for me.

"Fine. But only for a few minutes. I want to get you home so I can take care of you."

"Thank you!" I say as I sit up from the back seat and place a kiss on his cheek.

"Are you not buckled in? Sit your ass down and buckle up," he reprimands, and I just roll my eyes. Always so protective.

When we pull into Mill's parking lot, he puts the car in park and jogs around to my side, opening the door. I pull Gage out of his car seat and place a kiss on his forehead.

His hair is as dark as mine. He came out with a full head, and it's as black as a raven's wing. And although his eyes are that newborn gray, I can see the shimmer of hazel in them, just like mine.

He is my little carbon copy.

"Angel? What are you doing here?" Ski exits the shop, meeting us out front. "You should be at home recovering."

"That's what I told her, Ski." Vincent narrows his eyes at me, but I ignore him.

Walking up to Ski, he continues his reprimands. "You really should get home, you—"

His eyes drop to my son, and I see his breath catch in his chest. He is stock-still, frozen in time with eyes glued to Gage.

"He's—"

"Perfect." I finish for him. "Do you want to hold him?"

"I've never held a baby. I don't want to break him." He shakes his head and takes a small step back. This grumpy, 6'3" Devil dog, scared of a little 7lb 8oz baby. I giggle as I take Ski's arm and show him how to position it. Then I gently lay Gage in one arm and then guide his other around so he cradles him.

I leave my hand resting on Ski's forearm, right over his Marine Corp tattoo. "See. He fits perfectly in your arms."

Ski's eyes haven't left Gage. "He looks just like you," he whispers. Then he traces the large, rough pad of his finger down the bridge of Gage's nose, and he wiggles in his swaddle. Scrunching up his nose at the sensation, Ski laughs. A laugh that rattles his entire chest.

"God, Angel. You did so good. Mills would have loved him."

"Vin, take a picture of us. The camera is in the car." My grumpy husband rolls his eyes, then turns and jogs to the car. I watch Ski hold Gage. I think about how he would have been an incredible father if he and Millie would have been able to have children. But Ski has adopted me as his own, just as Millie did, and I like to think that they feel as connected to me as I do them.

My own parents abandoned me at a safe house when I was just a baby, and I had been in and out of the foster system all my life. Typically, babies get adopted easily, but I was never that lucky. I went through quite a few families, but none were good, and I ran from most of them.

I began to dabble in drugs when I was fifteen, and it was Vincent who helped me. He saw me on the streets, and something about me drew him in...or so he says. He never gave up on me, and he helped me get clean. I owe him my life.

"Got it." Vincent holds up the camera, looking through the lens. "Ready?"

"Do you want to know his name?" I look up to Ski, and he meets my eyes.

"Of course."

"Gage Henry Eros."

A smile breaks out across Ski's face, and a tear falls from his eye. The camera flashes.

# Chapter Eighteen

## 2002

"Here, Angel. I found this in the back. Thought you might want it now that—" Ski drops his eyes, unable to look at me anymore. It's not out of disgust. He sees too much of Millie's last days in me now.

I take the beanie from his hands. Taking off the plain black knit that covers my head, I replace it with the deep plum one she used to always wear. "Thank you. I can still smell the hazelnut on it." I let out a small laugh.

The corner of Ski's lip tugs up. "Yeah."

He raps his knuckles against the counter. "Well. I have to go take care of some stuff in the back."

"Ski, wait. Do you mind helping me with something?"

Coming around from the counter, he scratches the back of his head. I'm sure he's nervous about what I will ask of him. We both know my days are numbered. The treatments had such little chance of working, and I'm getting weaker each day.

"Sure, Angel."

"I have something in the back of my car. Do you think you could run out and grab it for me?"

I barely managed to get it into the back of the car. My body is just too frail now. But I did it. I didn't want Vincent to know I was bringing it to Ski. I don't know what he would have done knowing Ski had something that meant so much to me. But that's why I need him to have it.

Vincent has been beside himself. He can't stand the idea of my death, but we both know my chances of survival are low. Too low. I see his mask falling, the darkness threatening to escape the shell of a man he has become. He's been more irritable, volatile even. I know he's scared.

When I'm gone, it will only be Gage and him. And I know he loves our son, but I didn't have time to put anything in place to protect Gage. And even if I had time to prepare, Vincent has never been a danger to us. I would have no grounds. But a pressure in my chest tells me something is off. Something is... I don't know. Maybe it's just the idea of dying that has me overthinking.

As Gage took more and more of my time as he grew, Vincent became...jealous. I could see it in his eye when he would look at Gage as I held him or bathed him. He even became angry when I started to cosleep with Gage, saying our bed was for us, "not that baby."

I'm scared of what will happen when I'm gone.

Will he hurt our son?

Ignore him?

Will he be there for Gage and raise him like we talked about?

That's why I need to bring Ski in. I need someone else looking out for Gage.

"Your typewriter?"

"Yes. I don't know what Vincent will do with my belongings, and this one is too important to leave it to his impulsive tendencies. I need you to give this to Gage when he turns sixteen."

Ski sets it on the counter and runs his finger over the custom arrow key I had put in. One of my foster sisters had told me about what the arrow means. The only way to shoot an arrow is to pull it backward, so when life pulls us back and we feel we aren't moving in the right direction, it's because it's preparing to let us soar into something great.

It's funny that I married a man with the last name Eros. Just seemed like fate at the time.

The typewriter is my one possession from my foster days. I found it in an attic at one of my temporary homes. I fixed it up and began writing on it. I used to type all of my hopes, dreams, frustrations, and sorrows. This old thing has seen my smiles, heard my laughter, soaked up my tears, and now it will do the same for my son.

"I'll make sure he gets it, and he knows who it's from."

"No."

His brows dent in. "What?"

"Don't tell him it's from me." I press down the arrow key, imagining Gage one day pressing down on this key to sign his letters. Will he write his college essays on it? Love letters to his soulmate? His wedding vows?

"I don't understand, Angel."

"Ski, I don't know who my son will be."

That's it.

He's only five.

I'm going to die before I see who he becomes.

I had been coping with all of this, but right at this moment, I just realized I won't know who my son will become. I won't see him play his first ball game. Graduate from high school. Fall in love. Fall out of love. I won't see him walk down the aisle. I won't see him kiss his bride or hold his first child. Will he even want children? Will he even marry? Will he be full of joy and laughter like I used to be? Will he be quiet and attach himself to one person like his father?

Will he allow himself to love after losing his mother?

"I don't know who my son will be." I break down, tears streaming down my face. Ski comes around and wraps his arms around me. I sob in his arms as he places a kiss on top of my head.

"Shhh. He will know, Evangeline. He will know. When he is ready. I will make sure he knows. I promise."

More sobs escape my body as my chest heaves. It hurts. God, it hurts so much. More than the cancer, more than the nausea and the vomiting, more than the headaches and the utter fucking physical exhaustion. What hurts is knowing that I will never know my son. He will never know me.

Will he have any memories of me?

"You can't tell him this is from me. Not until he is ready. I don't know who he will be and where he will be in his life at that time. If he's angry at the world, he may be angry with me, and he needs this typewriter. He can't get rid of it out of anger. If he is happy in his life, if all my prayers are answered, you tell him. I leave it up to you, Ski. Watch over him. Please."

"I'll do my best, sweet girl."

I dry my tears as best I can, wiping them away with the sleeve of my jacket. "I should get going. We are burying a time capsule at the elementary school, and... I want to be there."

"I'll see you after."

## ski | 2010

"What flowers you got today, Ski?" the caretaker asks as if he doesn't already know. It's always the same. Every Sunday. Always the same.

Their favorites. "Dahlias and lilies."

I set the lilies down in front of my Mill's headstone. "For you, księżniczka." Then set the dahlias on my Angel's. "Your favorite, sweet girl."

I slowly lower my old, tired body to the ground, resting between the two headstones. Thanking God that Evangeline had the sense to buy this plot before that damn husband of hers was able to dictate where she was buried.

She belongs with us.

And when my heart stops beating, I'll lie next to them. I've already purchased the plot next to Mills, and already bought my casket. I'm ready.

"I saw Gage today, Angel. He looks more and more like you each day. But he also acts like his father more and more." I shake my head because that has been the hardest thing to watch. My Angel's son turning out just like his father.

I reach out and brush off some dirt that had settled onto her headstone. I've kept my eyes on Gage like I promised, but he never comes into Mill's. I tried to go to his house to talk to him, but Vincent ran me off, threatening me with a restraining order. Lord knows he could get one without any proof. The damn man has all these dirty cops in his pocket, as well as the mayor.

But I still watch. Gage keeps his head down and doesn't talk to anyone but Everett, the mayor's son. At least he has someone. And that boy is good. Everett is nothing like his father. There is a light in him that radiates.

A light that Gage needs.

"I'm afraid, Angel. I'm afraid something is going on, and I can't protect him. But how can I fight Vincent? He's got too much power in this small town. I need you to pull your weight up there. Give him someone who sees him. Understands him. Someone he can confide in."

"Księżniczka, you're not off the hook either. I need some help, baby. I need a sign you're still with me because I'm losing you. You're drifting. Just like in Nam, when I began to forget. I'm forgetting, and maybe it's my old age... but maybe it's time I come home? Huh? Maybe it's time I come back to you. What else am I on this god-forsaken Earth for? Both my girls are gone."

I pull out my deck of cards and shuffle them in my hand. A habit I picked up in the war to distract my hands when all I wanted to do was take the gun and put it to my own head.

The habit I continued when I returned home and wanted to do the same thing.

But Millie remained relentless in her fight for me. The time my helo went down, and I was behind enemy lines for a whole week, the only thing that kept me hiking up that damn hill for rescue was her. The thought of never looking into her blue eyes, tasting her sweet lips, or holding her warm body. I fought for her. But now, I have nothing left to fight for.

"I've held on so long, księżniczka. You told me to fly, and I have been, but my wings are tired. I don't feel the wind beneath them anymore, so it's time. But if it isn't, if there is still a purpose of me being on this fucking planet without you, you gotta show me. Tell me. Talk to me, Mills."

The trees whisper as the wind blows through them. "Not clear enough, baby. I need you to be louder. I can't hear you."

I wait. And wait. And wait. But there is nothing.

Using Mill's gray stone to help me stand, I brush off my jeans and the top of each of their headstones.

"I'm coming back to you, Mills."

When I get back to the coffee house, the bell dings as I open the door, and I smile to myself as I remember Mill's pestering me about that damn bell for months until I finally got around to installing it. It's the most annoying fucking thing, and I think about smashing it with a hammer at least ten times a day but then I remember her.

Going to the back, I log into my email and type out the response to the real estate agent who thinks he has a buyer for Mills. I have everything taken care of. It's all aligned.

It's time to clean and oil my gun one last time.

Ding. Ding.

*That fucking bell.*

"Be with you in one moment," I say as I get up from my chair and make my way to the front.

A young girl waits at the counter, and when her bright blue eyes meet mine, the shiner on her left eye makes my blood boil. She can't be more than... thirteen or fourteen. But despite that, her eyes shine. Just like my Mill's.

My mind flashes back to when Evangeline walked through our doors. I can practically see Millie looking back to me with that look in her eyes, telling me that we are adopting this one too. Mill's little collection of broken souls, with me being her first.

"What can I get you?"

"Coffee. Please. With heavy cream."

"Have you ever tried it with the cream frothed? Adds a nice layer of foam on the top."

She looks at her feet like she isn't used to anyone conversing with her. "Sure."

"I'm going to add some cinnamon on top. You seem like you might like that."

She still hasn't looked up. "Okay."

"Can I get a name for the order?"

Now she looks up. Her eyes are fearful. Of me? Or of someone wanting to get close to her?

What would my Mills do right now? She'd probably smile and introduce herself first to make the little bird with a broken wing more comfortable.

"I'm Ski. And you?"

"Leora." Her timid voice breaks my heart.

*Protect her, Henry.*

*She's for my son, Ski.*

Dammit, girls. I was almost home.

After I give her the coffee, she goes to leave. When she opens the door, the bell dings again.

"Hey, Leora."

She turns, looking over her shoulder as her wild curls block half her face, block the bruise to her eye.

"Come back to me, okay?"

Her lips lift into a smile. "I'll see you tomorrow."

Ski & Millie

Henry Stephen Kwiatkowski – "Ski"

# Acknowledgments

A re you okay? Dry your tears, love. It's going to be okay. I promise.

There are many people I can thank for getting this story to print but the main one, is Henry Kwiatkowski aka Ski. My grandpa. Thank you grandpa for starting and feeding my coffee addiction at the fine age of 12 years old. Thank you for allowing me to sit silently with you when I needed, you never pushed or pried, you knew how healing silent company could be. Thank you for pulling out your deck of cards and leaving me with a wonderful memory of you every time I see someone shuffle a deck. And in a way, I guess I can thank you for me becoming an author because the first time I experienced how healing writing can be, how powerful it can be was when I wrote you a goodbye to read at your funeral. I see you in so many moments of my life.

For my readers, I want you to know how incredible this man was. The stories you heard in this book were real. The helicopter going down and Ski's one week journey behind enemy lines, the story of him standing in the front yard protecting those he loved, the deck of cards, the love for coffee, the Devil Dog tattoo. So much came from him.

In the books, you left a lasting impression on Leo and Gage...and even Natasha. But the real you, you are with me always.

I love you and miss you, you old grump.


Till our next escape,

–S

S. E. Emory is a contemporary romance author who enjoys writing heart-wrenching stories. She loves taking real life struggles and heartaches and creating the happily ever afters that we all deserve. S.E. enjoys playing with her two kiddos, watching anime with her husband, and sipping coffee in her rocking chair with a warm blanket and her latest all consuming read.

Connect with S. E. Emory online

www.seemorybooks.com

g
goodreads.com/seemorybooks

instagram.com/s.e.emory

tiktok.com/@s.e.emory

### Website

www.seemorybooks.com

### Instagram

www.instagram.com/s.e.emory

### Goodreads

https://www.goodreads.com/seemorybooks

### Pinterest

https://www.pinterest.com/seemorybooks/

### TikTok

https://www.tiktok.com/@s.e.emory